VARIATIONS ON THE BODY

VARIATIONS ON THE BODY

MARÍA OSPINA

Translated by Heather Cleary

COFFEE HOUSE PRESS

Minneapolis

2021

First English-language edition published 2021
Copyright © 2017 by María Ospina
Translation © 2021 by Heather Cleary
Cover design by Tree Abraham
Book design by Ann Sudmeier
Author photograph © Simón Parra
Translator photograph © Walter Funk

Vintage scissor images © karakedi35/Shutterstock.com
and paranormal/Shutterstock.com

First published in Spanish as *Azares del cuerpo* (Bogotá: Laguna Libros, 2017);
author represented by Casanovas & Lynch Literary Agency (Barcelona).

Coffee House Press books are available to the trade through our primary distributor, Consortium Book Sales & Distribution, cbsd.com or (800) 283-3572. For personal orders, catalogs, or other information, write to info@coffeehousepress.org.

Coffee House Press is a nonprofit literary publishing house. Support from private foundations, corporate giving programs, government programs, and generous individuals helps make the publication of our books possible. We gratefully acknowledge their support in detail in the back of this book.

LIBRARY OF CONGRESS CATALOGING-IN-PUBLICATION DATA

Names: Ospina, María, author. | Cleary, Heather, translator.
Title: Variations on the body / María Ospina ; translated by Heather Cleary.
Other titles: Azares del cuerpo. English
Identifiers: LCCN 2021009749 | ISBN 9781566896108 (trade paperback) |
    ISBN 9781566896146 (epub)
Subjects: LCSH: Ospina, María—Translations into English. | LCGFT:
    Short stories.
Classification: LCC PQ8180.425.S688 A9713 2021 | DDC 863/.7—dc23
LC record available at https://lccn.loc.gov/2021009749

PRINTED IN THE UNITED STATES OF AMERICA

28 27 26 25 24 23 22 21   1 2 3 4 5 6 7 8

33614082349993

To the memory of Gustavo Pesoa
and his polished murmur.

CONTENTS

TRANSLATOR'S NOTE: VARIATIONS ON THE VOICE

As its title suggests, María Ospina's kaleidoscopic first book of short fiction centers on the body. The female body, more precisely, situated in the interconnected but unequal urban space of Bogotá in the first decade of the twenty-first century. Though Ospina's keen eye for psychological detail allows the situations depicted in this collection to resonate with readers across place and time, the bodies that inhabit these fictions are very much of the years immediately following the escalation of violence in Colombia during the 1980s and '90s. Armed conflict in the country dates back much further, but these decades marked a massive surge in both the drug trade and the resources assigned to the putative war on drugs, itself inextricably linked to the spread of neoliberalism and the interventionist policies of the United States. The multiform and widespread violence between the State, paramilitary groups, and guerrilla fighters had a massive effect on the social and political landscape of Colombia: the militarization of the countryside forced millions to flee to the relative safety of the capital city, where they encountered different forms of violence, rooted in biases surrounding race and social class. Meanwhile, as Ospina observes in *El rompecabezas de la memoria* (2017), at the same time that hundreds of thousands of people were being wounded or killed, displaced, disappeared by the State, or recruited to join armed factions, the government was implementing initiatives that sought to promote reconciliation and the reintegration of former fighters into civilian roles.

The bodies in *Variations* bear the marks of this historical and interpersonal violence. In the first story, a former guerrilla fighter tries to scrub away a battle scar while getting used to the new, corporate set of orders she is expected to follow behind the register of a Carrefour megastore. In the second, a young woman finds that between the baby growing inside her and the child she is paid to care for—but who treats her like a plaything—her body hardly seems to belong to her; the child's mother, for her part, is left reeling when a friend is killed by a bomb planted on an airplane. Other stories feature a character obsessed with the flea bites that multiply nightly across her skin, teenage girls forced to navigate both their growing bodies and the eyes that fall upon them, women who alter their faces and physiques to various extremes—from waxing and clipping to surgical restructuring. These are bodies searching for connection and completion in a world that tends to slice up and serve: catcalls hail tits or ass; gender norms deride a muscular leg or arm; labor exploitation, fueled by racist othering, knows just what to do with the hands.

Just as each of the women who populate these stories finds her body at the nexus of different desires, expectations, subjugations, and hopes, so too does the voice of each narrative occupy specific social and political coordinates; in several stories, the voice itself is subject to physical and symbolic violence. One form this violence takes is silencing: when Marcela, the protagonist of "Policarpa," returns to the offices of the publishing house that has bought the rights to her memoirs of her time as a guerrilla fighter, she finds that her editor has dramatically altered her account to remove the texture of her experience— particularly her more lyrical reflections on birds—and all trace of her colloquial speech to better conform to the sensationalist expectations of the market. This stifling of Marcela's narrative is somatized as a powerful, recurring feeling of nausea— a symptom shared by her pregnant sister, Zenaida, in the following story.

Sometimes this violence is embedded not in censorship or appropriation but in the way a voice is penetrated by others. In "Occasion," the continual breaching of the boundaries of Zenaida's body by Isabela's tugging, unfastening, and untying is echoed in the instability of the narrative point of view: though it is ostensibly Zenaida's story we are following, we often slip into Isabela's version of events. These shifts sometimes occur even within the same paragraph and can sometimes be quite subtle (one clear marker, nonetheless, is the description of the woman of the house, which alternates between "mother" and "employer"). As we move into and out of Zenaida's subjectivity in this way, we grow increasingly aware of the porosity of the physical and psychological spaces afforded to her and, by extension, the precarity of her situation.

The next story, "Saving Young Ladies," offers another kind of polyvocality—perhaps the most challenging of the collection to translate. The protagonist, Aurora, has just moved back to Bogotá after years living in the United States and spends her days in intense solitude. The closest thing she has to a human connection, in fact, is the time she spends watching the comings and goings of the girls in a Catholic residence across the street from her apartment, where they live, study, and—if they choose—prepare to take their vows. Aurora becomes increasingly fixated on one of them, and increasingly determined to save her from her oppressive surroundings. This salvation, however, is tinged with erotic projections and curiosity and clearly responds far more to Aurora's emotional needs than to those of the girl she is trying to save.

The intermingling of spiritual salvation and erotic desire is reinforced by the story's central narrative conceit: sustained intertextual references to the poem "The Dark Night of the Soul" by San Juan de la Cruz. The poem, written in the late sixteenth century while the soon-to-be saint was imprisoned by his fellow Carmelites for being *too* fervent in his religious beliefs, traces the journey of a soul as it sheds its earthly yoke and unites with God's love, through the metaphor of a young woman who sneaks out of her house at night and travels through the dark to lay with her Beloved. This poem holds a mirror up to Aurora's conflation of desire, curiosity, and redemptive fervor, and its first verse appears in its entirety toward the end of the story, reframing the events that precede it. What might not be immediately apparent, however, to a reader whose early education did not include reading San Juan de la Cruz, is that Ospina weaves phrases and terms that point to this canonical poem throughout. The narrator's description of the "sosiego" she seeks, and that of the residence under her constant surveillance, corresponds to the phrase "estando ya mi casa sosegada" ("My house being now at rest"), which closes the first two stanzas of the poem and is the circumstance that allows the speaker to escape into the arms of her Beloved. The phrase is repeated in full toward the end of the story, the only difference being a shift from "my" to "her." In that same paragraph, the image of petting the stray dog's "flowery breast" is an echo of the speaker's "pecho florido," upon which the Beloved lays his head in the sixth verse of "The Dark Night of the Soul."

Intertextual references of this kind present an extreme example of Walter Benjamin's claim in "The Task of the Translator" (the preface to his 1923 translation of Charles Baudelaire's "Tableaux parisiens") that the German "Brot" cannot truly stand in for the French "pain," because each carries with them a constellation of cultural associations that push the chemically similar combinations of wheat, water, and leavening toward incommensurability. If the ways in which bread is made, sold, shared, and eaten in two different sociohistorical contexts is enough to make us rethink what it means to reproduce a work across languages and time, this challenge will be even more pronounced when it comes to references made to a text that is canonical in the translated language but not widely known in the translating one. This is doubly true when multiple translations exist of the text being invoked: not only will the resonance and associations necessarily be different, if the reference is caught at all; due to these competing versions it becomes nearly impossible to pinpoint those words that evoke or harmonize with the poem. Thankfully, we have translator's notes to point out these gestures—and, hopefully, the spirit of the references can be felt in the intermingling of erotic and religious language, even without the detective work of going back to see which words from the quoted verse at the end of the story appear throughout.

Even when told in the third person, each of these stories has its own voice—a voice tied to the bodies that move through the collection, interacting in different contexts and roles. Sometimes the difference is pronounced, as in the visual effects of "Policarpa" and the comical use of the first person in "Fauna of the Ages." Sometimes it is quite subtle, as in the collection's final two stories. Challenging the categorical moral and political narratives so often imposed on this complex historical moment, Ospina's variations on the voice offer us a glimpse of Bogotá as a multifaceted microcosm of interconnected worlds.

Heather Cleary
Mexico City, October 2020

VARIATIONS ON THE BODY

POLICARPA

Not being devoured is the most perfect of feelings.
Not being devoured is the secret goal of an entire life.

— Clarice Lispector, "The Smallest Woman
in the World" (tr. Katrina Dodson)

She scratches the ridge of her spine, right where the tag of her uniform is torturing her skin. It feels good. She digs around back there as her coworkers, assembled at the entrance to the superstore, applaud enthusiastically. She claps, too, until she stops to scratch again. She rejoins the daily ritual of customer appreciation just as the crowd begins to disperse. An old man struggling to push his cart along the aisle is the last of the shoppers who got up at the crack of dawn to take advantage of the store's First Saturday discounts. She studies her coworkers' lips, watching for the exact moment when their welcoming smiles fade, when their supply of celebratory gestures runs out. Her eyes bore into the other two women who started there recently, like her, but they seem to find nothing strange about any of it. Everyone goes back to their workstations.

Diana, the cashier assigned to train her at the register, walks up to her. Each woman reads the other's name on the tag pinned to her chest.

"Hey, Marcela. Let's get started."

She likes hearing her name again after so long. But it hasn't been easy to get used to. She needs to practice every day, saying

Marcela, Marcela, Marcela to herself, over and over. Now Diana is saying it, and she likes that. Diana might even become a good friend one day. The two squeeze into a small booth facing one of the registers.

"They're not that hard to use, but everyone makes mistakes the first few weeks. You might forget the code for a vegetable or something, but you'll be fine if you've worked in retail. What did you do before?"

"I cleaned offices."

It's the first thing she thinks of. The only office she knows in Bogotá is the publishing house on the seventh floor of a building on the corner of Eighty-Fifth and Eleventh. She's only gone there a few times to meet with her editor. They ask every time for photo ID at the entrance, and she takes out the shiny new card with her real name on it, then presses her finger to a machine taught to recognize her prints. One could say she works there, but not cleaning, and not full time. One could say her job is to reveal her identity.

The people at the Agency told her right away not to say anything about her journey (that's what they call it, which she finds a little strange) for at least the first few months. The advice seems obvious, but she doesn't know what to say when someone pries into the hidden corners of her past. In the harsh light of the superstore, she scolds herself for improvising and scratches her neck again, where the nylon tag itches her relentlessly. Then she bites off a piece of the dry crust that has covered her lips since she moved to Bogotá.

Diana starts up the register. She punches in a few zeros. The cash drawer pops open and hits their stomachs.

"Why'd you leave that job?"

"Ugh, it was the worst. The hours were long and the pay was awful. The way they exploited us, I almost went nuts."

"Yeah, well, it's getting harder and harder to find decent work. Where are you from?"

"I grew up in Teorama, a little town in Norte de Santander. But I've been working in Bucaramanga and Bogotá forever."

She gives the true part of the answer proudly, ignoring the psychologist's advice. In the first group therapy session the Agency organized, they were told to imagine their journey as a natural transition. Something as inevitable as a snake shedding its skin. That's how the psychologist put it, adding that prudence was key in the first phase of their return.

The sirs and misses brought into their therapy sessions (accustomed to the symmetry promised by the word *comrade,* she finds it funny that everyone here is "sir" or "miss") utter *jungle* and *mountain* cautiously, seriously, the words heavy enough to shut down conversations on the spot. Hearing them talk, Marcela feels like a warrior swinging from vines in a wilderness full of predators.

Standing with her hip pressed against Diana's at the cash register, Marcela thinks that if they grow closer one day and she decides to tell her everything, Diana will ask her about animals, weapons, trees, and danger. And probably about how closely she lived with death. She imagines feeling overwhelmed, unsure how to explain it all. She imagines Diana struggling to understand the shards of the story she reluctantly offers and trying to decide whether or not they could ever be friends.

In the Health and Beauty department, which she was assigned to so she could familiarize herself with the products, Marcela learns about exfoliation. The first time she sees the word on the bottle of a soapy liquid gleaming with promise, she hunts for a definition on the label. Then she buys one that claims to scour away impurities and applies it with discipline every morning to the raised scar that interrupts her shoulder. She wants to sand down the pinkish mark so the wound won't reveal as much. Whenever the psychologist talks to them about their journeys in the Agency's group therapy sessions, Marcela thinks of those impurity-scouring soaps. She imagines them gradually sloughing away her one and only skin.

Since she began working at the superstore, she buys something from Health and Beauty almost every day. Whatever seems new and interesting. Tinted moisturizer, hair-removal kits, neon nail polish and a bottle of acetone, oatmeal facial soap. The jars don't all fit on the lone shelf in her room.

Since she began working at the superstore, she's also been having dreams about her dog. In the worst one, a pit viper bites her right on the nose. Marcela witnesses the attack but can't do anything to stop it. The skin on the little animal's face slowly dries up and peels away while she's still alive, until her head is nothing but bones. Marcela tries to save her by collecting every piece of skin, every whisker, that falls to the ground. Her sister helps her attach them again with a glue they pick up at the store, but her sweet little dog dies on them.

—

At their third meeting, Marcela's editor hands her a stack of paper. The first draft of her unfinished manuscript.

"All right, Marcela," she says. "Let's see what you think about this part. It's a transcription of what you've told us with a few changes I made for clarity and flow. There's still a lot of polishing to do and details to fill in. Read it and let me know if it looks good to you, or if you have a problem with any of my cuts or additions."

Marcela takes the mass of pages and begins to read out loud. The editor follows along on her screen.

> ~~At the start~~ Initially, when I started thinking about ~~leaving~~ my departure, I figured I'd write the whole way because I'd heard about people who had gotten out and told their stories and I thought ~~that telling~~ it would help untangle everything that ~~jams up your~~ occupies a person's ~~head~~ mind at times

like that. ~~And~~ I also wanted to have a written record. If I died along the way, I wanted at least to leave my ~~story~~ testimonial behind, so someone out there would ~~get~~ understand who I was and what I went through. ~~You know?~~

"I'm going to stop you here for a moment, Marcela. I'd like to know if this diary actually exists. It wasn't clear in our first interview."

"No. In the end, I didn't write a word. Imagine keeping notes on a trek like that. But I've got the diary right here in my head, clear as day, and I think that's maybe even better."

Marcela remembers a novel she hasn't read but that she's been told about in detail. It's about a poet who gets lost in the jungle and leaves behind a long manuscript about the violence and exploitation he witnessed on the rubber plantations of the Amazon. The woman Marcela had been ordered to care for back there had told her everything that happened in the book over the course of a week. She said it was her favorite novel. Whenever she'd beg them to give her something to read, she'd insist on that book. The commander would snap at her, "What do you think this is, a library?" Until Marcela talked to the higher-ups and managed to get her a Marxist pamphlet, a Bible, and a textbook on Colombian geography, which the two of them later read and discussed. "The problem is that novels aren't made for the jungle," the woman said to her one day. Marcela hadn't understood why she was laughing.

"The novel is called *The Vortex*, miss. I don't remember the author's name, but he's famous. Could you tell me where I can buy a copy?"

The editor promises to get her one. Marcela goes on reading the heavily edited manuscript.

I carried a notebook with me ~~for many years there~~ from the start. I'd draw things in it ~~(I've loved to draw, ever since I was a little girl)~~, jot down important dates ~~like birthdays or~~

~~when I lost someone close to me~~, start letters to my mom or my sisters, and write poems. I was going to leave it as a keepsake with Erika, my best friend back there, ~~like a sister or something, that's what she was,~~ but in the end I decided to bring it with me on this ~~last trip~~ adventure. ~~They say~~ It seems Erika deserted, too, but some people say she died in combat in Nariño. ~~That's something I'll figure out, now that I'm here. If she's alive, I've got to find her.~~

~~So, yeah,~~ All those years, I ~~was dying~~ wanted to send letters to my mom and my sisters. But I never did. The only letter I ~~sent~~ dispatched in all that time was to high command, to request some special medical tests because I ~~was all skin and bones~~ had lost a lot of weight and was getting weaker by the day. That was about four years after I joined, when I was about to turn twenty. The commander told me it was nothing, that I just needed to eat more. But I was eating fine and still losing weight, ~~right,~~ and my legs were always shaky. ~~And~~ So they sent me to Villavicencio, to a house they have for medical treatment, and they ran tests on me and ~~said, like, you have~~ diagnosed me with a thyroid problem. I wrote a lot while I was shut in there. ~~Can you imagine?~~ They'd left me ~~lying there~~ in a city I didn't know, ~~and my only company was~~ in the care of a woman who barely spoke and only came upstairs to bring me food. ~~There was nothing there but, like, a television and an annoying rooster that crowed nonstop down in the garden.~~ It was terrible.

~~Back then, I had a little dog. She took a shine to me in a settlement near Miraflores. I loved her to pieces. But then when she'd been with me a year the fighting started up again nearby and we had to break camp. I left her with some folks from Mocuare. It broke my heart to leave her behind, I was a wreck. I even wrote her a letter, I wrote to a few of the dogs from when I was a kid. I swear to God, though, one day I'll go back for her.~~

Marcela looks up from the paper but avoids the editor's eyes. Then she goes on reading.

Being shut in like that for two weeks was what made me so desperate to contact my mother and my sisters Nubia and Zenaida, ~~and say~~ to tell them I was okay, even though it had been a long time since they'd heard from me. ~~I think~~ I wanted them to know I was ~~here, I mean, living in this world, close to them~~ alive. I was always worried that they would get used to ~~the idea I was dead or lost~~ my absence, like happens to so many families ~~who get used to it and that's that. I didn't want them to bury me in their minds.~~ I wrote them a ~~really~~ long letter, ~~and I swear I meant to send it to them~~ but then I tore the pages out of my notebook and burned them. I knew ~~there was no way they'd let me~~ we weren't allowed to contact our families under any circumstances. They'd caught Katy and Edwin, two of my ~~comrades~~ friends from training, early on, and the punishment was ~~rough~~ severe.

Marcela sets the last printed page at the top of the stack of paper on the desk. The editor raises her eyebrows, waiting for her approval.

"It's fine. You know, I remember when I burned that letter—I remember wanting to mix the ashes in a glass of water and swallow them. But instead I threw them out the window to see if the rooster would eat them and hold onto the memory for me."

She laughs. The editor does not.

"Was that the first time you lived in a city?"

"Yes, but I barely saw any of it. As soon as I got better, they sent me back to the camp. My dad took me to Cúcuta once when I was little, but I don't remember it."

"Perfect. I'm going to add in a few sentences explaining that. Too bad you didn't keep any of those papers, Marcela.

Imagine being able to include reproductions of your words in this book, written in your own hand, to underscore how heroic it was that you were writing from the jungle. So. You approve my edits to this section, Marcela?"

"Yes, miss. I approve."

"Next week, when the transcript is ready, we'll go over the details of your forced recruitment. That needs to be a separate chapter and should come before what we reviewed today."

"I signed up, no one forced me. You can't change that part."

"All right. You can tell me all about it next time."

Night is falling when she steps into the street. Between two buildings she catches sight of the mountain tangled in clouds. A fog of uneasiness settles over her skin, and she doesn't know where she can go to scrub it off. The editor had told her from the start that they would cut and change much of the original transcription. They'd even made her sign a consent form. But she'd rather not witness the crossing out and cutting and condensing, so she's decided to keep a few things to herself. She won't mention her silent devotion to the birds she studied for years, how she deciphered their rituals and migration patterns, drew them in her notebook, invented names for them. Or how she would imagine what they saw from up in the trees when the bombing and the shooting intensified. What must have echoed in their hearts with every explosion. None of that deserves to be crossed out.

Marcela walks a while before catching the bus, to see if she can get some blood flowing through her hips and buttocks and all the other flesh not yet accustomed to her new urban stasis. She begins the hectic march that she's grown used to by now, keeping an eye out for the buses spewing billows of smog at the sidewalk. She waits for the thick air to make its way up the street in the futile hope of avoiding it. Other times, she breaks the straight line of her steps and twists her path away from the metallic cloud that seeps into everything, trying to avoid contact. She holds her breath for ransom as she tries to keep out the smoke that burns her throat, makes her sneeze, irritates her eyes. Do the birds feel its heat? She figures she'll eventually be able to ignore these little eruptions, like everyone else who moves through the city looking more or less composed.

—

Every so often she finds a moment to stare at the superstore's white metal and cement ceiling. Her eyes rest on the bareness of its panels, interrupted by metallic cylinders, cables, smoke detectors, and cameras. She likes to look up at it every morning, as if to escape the fiction of buying and selling. To remind herself that everything stacked orderly under the flat roof—the aisles full of strategically lit products, the signs, the applause—is just a fleeting topography of crates and calculations. The artifice of abundance. It amazes her, how the merchandise so effectively veils the crude box that is the warehouse. Looking up has become her ritual.

She works slowly at the cash register. Too slowly, Diana says from time to time, trying to hurry her up. But Marcela pays attention to every detail, scrutinizing each product, studying each package, repeating the names of foods she has never seen before and which she wonders if she might one day be able to buy. Dog treats shaped like bacon, peach-flavored vitamin powder, Band-Aids with cartoon monsters on them, unfamiliar vegetables, cheeses with foreign names, gringo creams and soaps. The universe of commodities, as the Marxist pamphlets say. She is surprised at how little the other cashiers seem to care about the hidden anxieties revealed by the contents of each shopping cart. She doesn't try to hide the fact that she eavesdrops on the customers' conversations, and they don't seem to notice. She stares at them like a young girl studying everything an older one wears and says. With brazen fascination, but also a kind of reverence.

—

It had been less than a day since I'd left the camp, and I
was ~~beat~~ exhausted. But I couldn't stop to rest because
I was ~~scared shitless~~ afraid they were going to catch me.
By that point in the morning, they must have realized I
~~was gone~~ had deserted and ~~you can bet your ass they~~ had
probably sent a few of the others after me. I'd left around
three, after my shift on watch, in the middle of a ~~crazy~~
heavy storm. I ran for a few hours along a narrow path
before I reached a stream that leads to the Nukak Reserve.
We'd taken that same path a few days earlier, when they
sent us to find ~~food~~ snakes because we were running out
of things to eat.

"This part about the snakes isn't true, miss. Did you add
that in? They sent us for fish because we'd been eating nothing
but rice for weeks."

"I wanted to get your approval specifically on that change. I
think it's more impactful this way. Besides, I've read accounts
of combatants hunting serpents when their camps were running low on food. And you saw dangerous snakes, didn't you?"

Marcela's feet hurt. She hasn't gotten used to the long hours
standing still at the register. It feels good to take her shoes off
under the desk. Without answering the editor, she begins reading again.

The fighting had been so intense that we'd spent two
weeks hungry, nervous, on edge. I remember ~~chatting~~
talking with some of the others about how in the radio
interviews they did with people who'd deserted, some of
them said that what made them ~~finally~~ decide to run in the
end was that their hunger was ~~out of control~~ so severe. It
actually worked out well for me that no food was getting
through because everyone's morale was low. The ~~only snag~~
problem was that I didn't have much ~~to stash away~~ for the

trip either. After that first night away from the camp, ~~not long before~~ as the sun ~~was rising~~ rose, I realized I was on top of a ridge and that I had ~~covered~~ traveled ~~some serious~~ a great distance. ~~A shit ton.~~ Much more than I'd thought.

"I have a question about this part. Let's see if we can get a little more specific. How far do you think you traveled on this first stretch? The more details you can provide, the more realistic it will seem."

"With the twists and turns and all that, I'd say about six hours."

"If I show you a map, do you think we can be a bit more precise? We'll have one at the beginning of the book so we can show your exact route."

The editor turns her laptop around. Marcela sees her own reflection in its screen before her eyes focus on the image, a photograph of a surface made up of different shades of green, interrupted by brownish gray splotches and white tufts. A brown line snakes haphazardly through the anodyne vegetation of the jungle. Written across it are the words *Río Inírida*. The erratic river clashes with the simplicity of the landscape: its contours seem too alive, too winding and evasive, against the static image of the flatland.

"Whoa. Now that's a map . . . look at those colors, everything. It's a satellite image, right? I can't recognize anything like that, though."

"Hold on, I'll zoom in and show you up close."

The map gradually reappears on the screen. This time, its greenery is blurred, the river's curves less urgent. The picture vanishes again and is replaced by an indecipherable array of green and brown splotches.

"Now I *really* can't see what's what. No, wait. I know what that is—military camo, right?"

Marcela laughs. The editor does not.

"I zoomed in too far and the image blurred."

When the map appears again, Marcela recognizes a few names: Río Inírida, El Retorno, Morichal, Puerto Macaco, El Olvido, La Libertad. Thanks to her friendship with the camp's radio operator, who was also in charge of the GPS, she always knew the names of the towns, villages, and gullies they passed. It had seemed important to memorize them. She wrote them in her notebooks. But now, on the screen, she sees names she doesn't know: Sabanas de La Fuga, El Resbalón, Isla El Remolino.

"At that point we were near El Olvido, in the zone controlled by Comandante Danilo and the Thirty-Third Front."

Her finger grazes the computer screen, and she is surprised by the distortion it produces. She apologizes.

"But to say how many kilometers it was, just like that, I don't know. I was looking for one of the bigger lakes that form off the Inírida on Nukak land. I heard a special unit of the Omega task force was operating in the area, and I was betting on that. Those might be the lakes, there."

This time she just points, keeping her finger far from the screen.

"But I really can't say anything for sure from this map. . . . My eyes were on the ground the whole time, figuring out where to step, looking for paths. How do you think I'm going to be able to tell you what's what from the air?"

"I'm going to say thirty kilometers. It might be off by a little one way or the other, but at least it gives us an idea."

Marcela nods. She looks out the window at the mountains, their lines suddenly clearer now that the fog has lifted.

"Sabanas de La Fuga. What a perfect name. Wish I'd known I was running across the plains of escape."

—

Marcela hears the clack of a woman's high-heeled shoes approaching. A tall man with a dark mustache wearing a suit and tie walks beside her, pushing a full cart that he parks at Marcela's register. He might be a bodyguard or a driver, or both. He passes Marcela a few artichokes (she's just learned the code for those), a box of rice with words in a different language on it, and a slimy bag filled with rings of white flesh. She studies the name on the outside: *squid*. She likes how soft the cool flesh feels and gets an urge to pinch it like she does with the little plastic bubbles of the packing wrap she steals from the storage room, exploding each one between her fingers on the endless bus ride home. The man's tiny boss watches from a moderate distance as he and Marcela perform the choreography of commerce.

Marcela studies every detail of the minuscule woman. Her hair is dyed a pale blond and is suspended in a lacquered bubble; its solidity and airiness is startling. She wears big rings on her fingers and gold bracelets that jingle with her every movement, amplifying her wealth. A light layer of makeup helps conceal her thin skin and those reddish freckles blonds get. To hide her curiosity (Diana has told her that the customers hate to feel like they're being inspected), Marcela lowers her gaze every so often to the bar codes. When she looks up again, she studies the woman's hazel eyes and the way their freckled irises sparkle against their worn, gelatinous beds. She feels a whip crack in her throat. It's the green of those eyes. She imagines the woman dressed in sweats with the white hair of someone who hasn't been to the salon in a long time, sitting on a tarp under the trees that grow along the Guaviare, discussing a Marxist pamphlet. Marcela thinks she might vomit, right there in front of the golden mass of that woman standing with her wallet open, ready to pay for her purchases. Right there in front of the woman's driver, who handles everything.

"Do me a favor, Diana, and ring this ticket up? I don't feel so good."

She gives the little door that holds her captive at the register a hard push. An ethereal wave of vomit surges up a tube deep inside her, much deeper than her throat. The old woman manages to catch her profile, the snug blue uniform, the tight bun all the women who work at the superstore are expected to wear. She watches her disappear down the sale aisle.

"What's wrong with her?"

For a moment the man beside her is transformed from a domestic helper into a bodyguard and turns down the aisle to see where the checkout girl is headed.

—

I could have gone on walking, except I risked running into members of the other front, which was ~~trading fire~~ locked in combat with one of the ~~enemy's~~ army's mobile units. Maybe they'd already figured out I'd defected, but I knew their orders were to defend against the ~~enemy~~ army above everything else. I heard shots and voices and a couple of army helicopters flying overhead ~~and~~. So I hid in a ~~shack~~ little cave formed by a few fallen trees. ~~To be honest,~~ Though I wasn't sure they were looking for me, ~~but~~ I spent the whole afternoon of that first day tucked away in there, not moving, waiting for the sun to ~~go down~~ set so I could take the path to a lake I'd seen on one of our reconnaissance missions. My plan was to swim across it if I could.

"I think we should add something here about food. If you went hungry, if you had to find nourishment in the jungle."

"In my backpack I had some raw sugar, cooked rice, and two sausages I'd stolen from the kitchen back at camp. The plan was to ration them and eat them later, depending on how hungry I got. On the third day I decided to eat two fat caterpillars I found in the hollow of a tree trunk. No idea what they could have been. They were bright green and covered in bristles. I was worried they might be poisonous and thought to myself, what if I end up with my tongue all paralyzed? But I took a chance and wolfed them down, pretending they were pork rinds. And look at that, I'm here to tell the tale. Actually, they were kinda good."

"Perfect. I'll add that in, then, if you don't mind."

The editor is taking notes on her computer. Marcela feels a rush of pride at having come up with such a believable lie. She imagines the caterpillars, which she's never tasted and never will, crunching across the pages of her book forever. And the readers, wrinkled in disgust.

—

After the daily ritual of customer appreciation, Marcela goes to see the floor manager, who has called her into his office.

"I'm told this is the third time you've left the register in the middle of your shift. I'll remind you that every absence during working hours must be accompanied by a doctor's note. If this continues, your absences will be deducted from your paycheck as time not worked. More than three absences is grounds for dismissal. It's all in your contract. You did read the contract, didn't you?"

"I'm sorry, sir. It's true that I've stepped away briefly from the register for minor health issues, but I always come back quickly. Don't worry, sir. It won't happen again."

She's been using the word *sir* a lot lately. She doesn't like it, but she uses it. To tame it. Just like she does with her old name.

"It concerns me that you keep leaving the customers hanging with their purchases. Listen, we've welcomed you folks in the reintegration program with open arms. It's part of Carrefour's social mission and our commitment to peace. And I congratulate you personally on your decision to leave the jungle behind. But I must remind you that here, we work on a schedule, and each employee is responsible for her own discipline as part of her commitment to the company. No one is forcing you to be here, it's not like back there."

Marcela scratches near her sternum to interrupt the manager's gaze, which is fixed on her chest. Before leaving the area where the offices are for the giant warehouse of products on display, she stops to observe a plaque celebrating the employee of the month and a large aerial image of an agricultural field divided by neatly hewn paths. The slogan written across the poster is meant to be inspirational. "Carrefour: At the Crossroads."

—

~~Right, so anyway, when~~ When it started getting dark, I followed the path a little further until I ~~saw~~ recognized a field where we'd laid mines a few weeks earlier. I'd been in charge of the operation, so I knew the terrain. ~~So~~ I thought to myself~~, you're going to blow your legs off if you~~ that it would be too dangerous to try to cross it in the dark, and I decided to wait until daybreak. I dragged ~~a whole bunch of~~ branches over to the trunk of a tree and spent the whole night there~~, I mean, what else was I supposed to do. I think~~ I slept a little. At dawn, as I continued ~~on my journey~~ my escape, I saw that a large animal had been killed by one of the mines. It looked like a jaguar, but ~~I couldn't say for sure because~~ by then it was ~~just meat~~ carrion. ~~It made me so sad, so angry with myself because what did he have to do with the war. I even thought about staying to bury him, but that would have been irresponsible and so I kept going.~~ The path brought me to a big, beautiful lake that I recognized because we'd passed it a few weeks earlier ~~and I remembered thinking how pretty it was~~. I'd needed to help carry the ~~prisoner in my care~~ person we'd kidnapped when we crossed it coming the other way.

"All right, Marcela. This seems like a good time to remind you that we need more details about your relationship with the kidnapping victims."

"I told you before that I only saw a few right at the end, around six months before I left. I never wanted anything to do with that."

"But it's something people want to read about. People want to know if you got close to any of them. The whole thing about the older woman you cared for has to be in here. Try to give us more details."

"There was this one political prisoner they brought to the front for a few weeks, but then they moved him to another camp, and later I found out he'd been executed when the fighting started over there. We never spoke. In the end, they ordered me to watch over a woman who was called Doña Helena, or I should say, who is called that, since I figure she's still alive. She was old already and had been detained for six months by the time they ordered me to look after her. Jenny, who always cared for the detainees, had been wounded in combat. They picked me because I'd been in the unit longer than almost anyone. You have no idea how hard it was for me to accept the assignment. It was a job I'd always tried to avoid."

"Why?"

"Because I knew it would mess me up to see a detainee suffer up close like that. The others never talked about it, the subject was off-limits, but I knew it wrecked even the toughest ones, even if nobody was willing to admit it."

"As if you sensed you might realize that you were a captive too."

"I mean, maybe. . . . But you can't really compare one thing with the other, since I was the one who was holding the keys, right?"

"Right, but weren't you following orders too?"

"Anyway, in the end, it was being with her that gave me the push I needed to leave. She was actually the one who convinced me to go."

"Who was she?"

"They said she was from a family that owned a bunch of factories, but she never wanted to talk to me about any of that. And I never asked. She'd complain to me that her family had already sent piles of cash to pay the tax and she wasn't being released.

The handler assigned to her before me had been tough on her and threatened to confiscate the notebooks she'd managed to get her hands on. But we were close right from the start. We talked about lots of things, about our families. She told me about her children, I told her about my sisters, we even talked for hours about birds. She was an expert. Ever since I arrived, I'd been drawing the birds I saw in my notebook, so I'd show them to her and she'd tell me what they were called and sometimes even give me their scientific name—their elegant name, I call it. Sometimes she didn't recognize the birds in my drawings and she'd get really excited and ask me to describe them in more detail. She even told me that I had to make my escape when the big migrations were happening because the birds traveling together could be like a compass for me so I wouldn't get lost. While I was taking care of her, she turned seventy-two and I made her a cake. I got her pain pills, too, for her arthritis. I think she felt better around me, like she wasn't so alone, poor thing. In the end, I managed to leave her my radio to remember me by."

"And she knew you were leaving?"

"We'd started to trust each other more, and I tried to convince her to come with me, but we both knew she wasn't up to such a rough journey. Especially with the pain she had. She'd say to me, 'Poli, why are you still here? Scoot, darling.' I always thought they'd release her before I ran, which is why I had her memorize the names of my sisters and my mom so she could go find them and tell them I was all right, that I was alive, that they should wait for me because I was on my way. But go figure, I was the one who went first, and I didn't even have time to say good-bye."

The editor takes notes.

"Do you know if she's back now?"

"I don't know. No idea. I hope so. Poor thing."

She feels an overwhelming urge to tell her editor about the old woman in the superstore but catches herself in time.

"Anyway, none of this goes in. It's one thing for me to tell you the story like this, but none of it's going in."

She keeps reading.

~~Yeah, of course~~ I'd come across alligators in rivers and swamps a few times and figured there were probably lots of animals in the lake, and tons of snakes ~~too~~. So I tried not to think about that ~~and~~ while I swam across ~~like a shot~~ as quickly as possible. ~~Somewhere around t~~ There I came across a little river, one of the ones that feed into the Inírida. On the other side, two boys were out grazing their cattle. ~~I didn't know what to do until~~ I started waving to them, but they ran off ~~in a flash~~ as soon as they saw me. When I crossed the river, I ~~thought I~~ heard the motors of a few boats and that scared ~~the shit out of~~ me. I ran away from the river ~~forever~~ for about an hour until I found ~~a trench~~ cover under another fallen tree. ~~and~~ I stayed there a few hours. ~~and~~ Then it began to pour, and I thought I'd ~~try my luck~~ make the most of it and walk toward where I thought the army was, ~~since I'd figured out~~ taking into account the direction of the helicopters that had just flown ~~over me~~ overhead ~~were going~~.

—

"Have you decided when you're going to call your sisters?"

Diana likes to talk to her when they assign them neighboring cash registers.

"I don't know. This week for sure, I think. But only Zenaida, not Nubia. And not my mom, not yet. I couldn't call her without talking to Zenaida first."

They'd recently brought a woman who had fought with the M-19 guerrilla before joining the Ministry of Defense into the therapy sessions at the Agency. Wrapped in the dark fabric of her business suit, the woman told them about her return to Bogotá after years of fighting in Cauca. She had nearly committed suicide when the children she hadn't been able to raise bombarded her with questions just days after she arrived. But then she dug deep and found the strength not to kill herself. By way of a conclusion, the psychologist wrote on the board, "IMPORTANT: do not contact your family before a reasonable amount of time has gone by." Marcela had wanted to ask what a reasonable amount of time was but didn't dare.

"You have to let it go, Marci. It's been a long time, I'm sure they'll forgive you. Mothers forgive everything, you know."

She likes that Diana calls her Marci. It makes her feel young, like when she was in school in Teorama. She gets a sudden urge to tell her everything, like an avalanche. She feels it rise in her throat but holds back.

"Hey, Di. What happened with that bedding set? Is your aunt going to lend you the money for it? I can go with you to pick it out if you want."

She likes addressing Diana informally, though she senses they're still a long way from the friendship they've been building little by little, in the momentary truces granted to them by the customers and machines.

—

"Marcela, I find myself needing to remind you, again, that this book needs more details about your love life. We have plenty of descriptions of your adventures and how hard it is to cross the jungle, and of the chaos and all that, but it won't be powerful enough without the emotional aspect. No one's going to want to read something so dry. Try and remember if there isn't something you can include. Think hard."

"Well, I did have a boyfriend there. I've never loved anyone as much as I loved him. They recruited him during a raid in Meta, and I helped him learn the ropes. We were together in secret for almost a year before they moved him to a different front because it was against the rules to be with someone in your own unit, and they suspected there was something going on between us. That was in 2006, I haven't seen him since. Later, I heard he'd been caught and was in jail in Popayán. I haven't gone to look for him yet, but I'm thinking about it. One day. I mean, I'm not still in love with him, but I do care."

There's a silence.

"But don't put that in. That doesn't go in. And I'm not sure I want to say anything else about my family, either. Or, I don't know. That's something we'd have to negotiate."

—

Marcela makes a long-distance call from the internet café next to the superstore. The Agency has given her a number where she can supposedly reach her mother. The unfamiliar voice of a young man announces the woman's absence.

"Hm. I'm calling from Bogotá with an important message for her. Who am I speaking with?"

"I'm her son. Who is this?"

It's the first time she's heard the voice of her little brother cradled in words. Rubén was only a year old when she left. On the spur of the moment she can't think of any name besides her alias to give, but she softens it. Poli. Then she reproaches herself for using it. She explains that she is a friend looking for Zenaida and Nubia.

"They live in Bogotá, but Zenaida has a cell phone. If you want, I can give you the number."

She writes it down in the new notebook she bought to draw, all over again, the birds she remembers from back there. Before she hangs up, she tells Rubén she hopes to meet him one day.

—

This time she doesn't tell her editor she's going to miss their meeting. After work she takes a bus downtown. She doesn't know the area yet, even though she's supposed to go twice a month for therapy and to get her stipend from the Agency. She never has time to stroll past the old graffiti-covered walls that catch her eye from the bus. Diana told her once that San Victorino had nice gifts for a good price—cheaper than at the superstore, even with their employee discount. She is startled by the rage she senses behind the shrill honking of cars and buses along Carrera Décima. Overwhelmed by the din of the loudspeakers announcing sales, she steps into the plaza. She has a hard time getting her bearings.

She takes shelter in a clothing store. The name on the awning reads *USA Fashion*. She tries to recall the secretariat's communiqués about imperialist capitalism, but the clothes gleaming on their hangers dilute her thinking. After making two rounds of the store, she tries on a few sweaters in royal blue, Zenaida's favorite color. Did they still wear the same size? Was this still her favorite color? She ends up buying one of them, along with a gold watch for herself and a white onesie with a bear hugging a heart printed on it. In case Nubia and Zenaida have babies or for whenever they do. Or in case some other relative has one in the future. Maybe Diana would decide to have a kid with her new boyfriend.

—

The phone rings. For the first time in her life, she leaves a message. (She'd asked Diana how to leave messages on a cell phone, hoping she would guess what was behind the question.)

"Hi, Zena. It's Marcela. I'm calling from Bogotá. I live here now, kiddo, for the last three weeks or so. I'm out. I know it's been a long time but, well, I'd like to see you all again. I'll try you again later. Bye."

She wishes she'd left a longer message to explain why she's not so far away anymore. On the wall across from where she's waiting for the bus, she makes out some graffiti that reads *coke diet, Diet Coke*.

—

The old woman's driver pushes a full shopping cart up to the checkout. That same tie, that same thick mustache he's worn these last three weeks. Marcela sets the Closed sign on her register and walks quickly toward the employee restroom. She thinks she passes the woman in one of the aisles. She leans over the sink to vomit, but all that comes up is an acidic saliva that takes her three tries to spit out.

That afternoon in group therapy, she works up the nerve to speak for the first time. She describes her frantic sprints down the aisles of the superstore. The psychologist encourages the others to respond. They look at one another, but no one says anything. The psychologist intervenes.

"You're not the only one who has these experiences, Marcela. They're a common effect of the post traumatic stress of war. The visage you think you see isn't really someone you know."

The word *visage* unsettles her. She's seen it on some of the creams and soaps she bought from the superstore. She thinks about how she's never used it in a sentence. At the end of the session, Marcela approaches the psychologist to ask about that stress she mentioned, what the symptoms are. To see if maybe she has it.

Sunday is the only day she doesn't have to deal with shopping carts or hear the cash register's trill echo in her head. No one lines up for the bathroom that early, so she can spend extra time in the shower. She shaves her armpits, then scrubs the scar on her shoulder with a bit of the exfoliant she bought and spreads the rest up toward her neck. She applies a special conditioner formulated to prevent hair loss, twice. She dries off and lets her hair hang loose, the way she wore it back when she left Teorama, even though she suspects more will fall out that way. Still naked, she sweeps up the strands she's left orphaned around her room during the week. She moves the cardboard boxes where she keeps her clothes to reveal the hair entrenched in the corners. She returns to the thought that one day she'll have a huge armoire with lots of drawers and a mirror inside one of the doors. An elegant piece made of fine wood like the one she saw on a hacienda she entered with her unit in Meta. She'd stick photos inside the other door (she is unsettled to realize that she has no idea where those photos would come from). She'd hang others on the walls in shiny frames, like the ones her editor has in her office. The psychologist keeps saying that they need to "come up with new dreams," and Marcela wonders if this is what she means. She has recently begun to identify certain things she lacks.

It's still early. She dusts off the hot plate she picked up at the pawnshop so she wouldn't have to share a kitchen with the others in her tenement and notices, again, the fragility of the cardboard box it rests on. As she mops the white tiles, her longing for the leaf-covered dirt floors of her past unsettles her. She repositions the thick pile of manuscript pages engulfing the plastic chair, and her eyes fall on the Agency's pamphlet about options for finishing high school. She reproaches herself for not having read it. While she straightens the sheets, she thinks that if Diana ends up asking her to go buy that bedding set with her, she might be able to get a quilt or something to mask the austerity of her cot. A nice, warm one to protect her from the cold she can't seem to chase from her feet. She suppresses her desire for heavy curtains, like the ones that arrogantly hide everything she might strain to glimpse inside the apartments of the oligarchs (the oligarchs controlled by the empire, as the manuals insist). One day, she thinks, she'll want a television. She has a few minutes left for cleaning, to dust off the books that her editor has been giving her but that she hasn't had time to read and has nowhere to keep. If she gets a few more, she'll be able to stack them into a bedside table for her alarm clock.

She still has half an hour, so she decides to walk to the spot they agreed on. She puts on a brand-new pair of silver shoes that she bought at the superstore with her second paycheck, though she suspects she'll be limping after a few blocks. City shoes are no match for feet forged on dirt paths. She chides herself for wishing she had her rubber boots again.

Maybe she should use the diminutive, like she always had, to make things less formal. Zenita, kiddo. A hug? Start off by giving her the gift? Tell her about the book? Promise her that everything will make sense when she reads it?

In the café she orders an herbal tea and sits down at a table facing the door. She blows hard on the liquid in her cup, making little whirlpools. She watches two men in cycling gear and a woman with a girl fresh from the bath come and go. She tries to focus on the game show playing on the TV, but her eyes keep drifting back to the door. She orders a roscón and breaks the pastry into pieces that she eats hastily, to finish before Zenaida arrives. She pulls the plastic sheet from the face of her new watch and folds it into a tiny square.

What if she doesn't come alone? What if Nubia is with her?

She waits for an hour and a quarter, staking out the door from her seat, alert to every bus that stops nearby. She stares at an old tree across the street and is moved by the way its swollen roots break through the sidewalk, contained and patient but also unruly. Does the tree miss the dirt, or does it go through life ignoring its absence?

She turns back several times as she walks away from the café, hoping that maybe Zenaida had just been delayed and she might catch her heading inside.

That night, Marcela stays up late going through the five approved chapters. On the manuscript's pages, she marks things she wants to ask her editor to change. But before going to bed she burns them in the shower and scatters the ashes from the window like an offering.

—

~~When we took off in the army plane that brought me~~
~~here I couldn't believe the view. Seeing the trees and the~~
~~countryside, the mountains, all from above really blew~~
~~me away and I started thinking about the birds, and how~~
~~they see the world different from us. The first time I saw~~
My first glimpse of Bogotá was from the air. I was amazed
how long the streets looked and how big the city seemed,
even from way up high. ~~I was also, I'm not sure how to~~
~~explain it, I was dying to see up close what they'd always~~
~~told us about class divisions in Bogotá, about the inequality~~
~~in big cities. I'd always thought things would seem so~~
~~clear from the air, but then I realized nothing was easy to~~
~~understand from up there, you know? It's hard to explain~~
~~the feeling I had.~~ Down here, the streets seem to have so
little to do with what I saw from up there. It surprises me
each time I think about ~~that damn landing~~ my arrival~~, and~~
~~by that I mean every day. Then~~ I thought about my sisters,
too, and wondered if they were somewhere in that giant
maze~~, had they forgotten me or did they still remember?~~
and whether they still remembered me. I sent them a
message from up there, ~~with my mind, to say I was there,~~
~~to wait for me because I'll see them in no time flat~~ letting
them know that I'd arrived and that we would see each
other very soon. Since I moved ~~to Engativá~~ here, I hear
lots of planes flying overhead, and the noise ~~scares the~~
~~crap out of~~ startles me sometimes. Right away, I get~~, like,~~
an instinct to ~~make a~~ run for ~~the nearest hideout~~ shelter.
That's what it's like when I'm walking down the street and
~~there's one of those truck bang things~~ a motor backfires:
my reflex is to get ready for an attack ~~and I reach for the~~
~~rifle I don't have anymore. And sure, sometimes I hear a~~
~~bird singing and that brings me right back there, in my~~
~~memory. I mean, I know these are different birds and that~~
~~there are less of them here, but at the same time I figure~~
~~some of them might be the same, that there must be some~~
~~birds that stop here on their way there, or the other way~~

~~around. I should find out. Sometimes I think that if I still had my notebook, the one with the drawings, I could compare the birds I drew there with the ones here, but too bad a couple army grunts took it from me when I turned myself in, supposedly because it might contain valuable information. I get so mad when I think about it. But yeah, I miss lots of things from there. The trees, for starters, it's crazy how much I miss them. I can't see a single one from the window in my room and that really brings me down and the psychologist tells me I should go explore the city's beautiful parks. Then there's my friends, and my dog . . . you have no idea. Of course, there's plenty I don't miss~~ too.

"All right. We're going to need to expand this part a bit to share what you like about the city, what's surprised you, and also to include a few details about your family situation as it stands now. You said you didn't visit anyone you knew when you came back."

"No. But I've seen my sisters a few times now, and they've told my mother I'm here. I'm even going to move in with Zenaida in a few months."

"That's wonderful news. I'm so glad. Why didn't you say anything about all this?"

"Because I don't want it going in the book. If you'd like, you can put in that I saw my family, but that's all. No details."

"Think about it, Marcela. It's absolutely crucial to round out the story. Imagine how excited your readers will be. At our next meeting, we'll need to record the last leg of your escape and what happened when you turned yourself in. The climax of the story. Take your time deciding how you want to narrate the part about your family."

"This is the climax."

Silence. Marcela tells her editor that she'll miss their next meeting, she's planning to visit her mother in Teorama. They agree to pick up again when she returns. She leaves the office completely sure that she'll never set foot inside it again, that she'll never again pass her new ID to the guard in the lobby or try to avoid his pawing when he takes it, that she'll never again read pages with words crossed out or list her experiences into a tiny recorder that promises to safeguard them all. She knows she won't be the author of a book. And that she won't be paid. She is relieved, in advance, that she won't need to scan the barcode of her own story when someone grabs it from the stands adorning the checkout lines at the superstore.

"The person you have dialed is not available. Please leave your message after the beep."

"Zena, it's me again. I guess you got tied up the other day and that's why you couldn't make it to the café. That's too bad. It's okay, though, don't worry. When I finally get a cell phone, I'll give you the number so you can call me directly, since I always have to call you from the street and you'll never reach me that way. Or I'll give you the address of where I'm living so you can have it and maybe stop by one day, whenever you can. Whenever you like, Zenita. Sundays I'm always there, I'm there all day because that's my day off. Anytime, sweetie, I'll be waiting for you."

She feels strange for having said *sweetie*. *Kiddo* would have been better, that's what she used to call her back in Teorama. She recites her address.

"Okay. I'll be waiting for you. Talk to you or see you soon, I hope. Bye. Take care, bye."

She dials again.

"Kiddo, I forgot to say that I work at the Carrefour in La Floresta. Monday to Saturday from seven to four thirty. You can find me there for sure, if you'd rather stop by there. Okay. This time for real. Bye."

After the morning applause, Marcela finds Diana and they walk to the registers together.

"So? I was thinking about you yesterday. Did your sister show up?"

"No, but I left her a message with my address. She'll come, I know her. This morning I had a feeling that today was maybe the day. But like you said, I have to be patient. Anyway, I'm sure I'll be able to introduce you to her soon. You'll love her."

Diana squeezes her arm encouragingly.

"Whoa, Marcela, you're pretty built! I don't know how you stay in that kind of shape. Don't tell me you're spending your paychecks at the gym."

Marcela feels a viscous urge to cry rising in her throat and is relieved Diana can't tell.

"How was the christening, Di? What did you end up giving your godson?"

"It was awesome. I got him a mobile with wild animals, and Daniel even found someone to cover for him, so he came with me. I introduced him to the whole family."

"That's so great. When do I get to meet him?"

Marcela immediately regrets saying this. What if Diana thinks she's being pushy? They've never actually hung out. The women step into their booths under the watchful eyes of their supervisor. He spends his days reprimanding them for chatting.

Marcela's first customer is an elderly woman accompanied by a young man who helps her empty a small shopping basket.

"You don't happen to sell books on dream interpretation, do you, hon? I thought I saw one here once."

Marcela replies that she doesn't know. The woman tells the young man about her most recent nightmare. She'd woken up one morning and her house was full of red fish. There were so many she could barely walk, so she decided to share them. But just as she was filling a bag to bring to her neighbor, the doorbell rang and there was the neighbor, who had come by to offer her some of the same fish because they'd taken over her apartment too.

"I didn't know what to do, dear. And to think, abundance is supposed to bring happiness."

Marcela scans a bag of rice, a few bananas, an enormous bottle of bodywash, glass cleaner, and a biography of the president. Nothing really worth noting. She watches as they leave the abundance of the superstore. Her neck cracks when she looks up at the ceiling. She stares at its tubes and pipes as she drops her head to one side, then the other, to get at the pain lodged there. She notices signs of a leak in a far corner. She makes a face at the security camera that's always trained on her.

A woman walks toward her along the center aisle, holding a little boy's hand. Marcela notices the bright lettering on her low-cut T-shirt: SPECIAL BEAUTY. Underneath, an eagle in flight like something out of a military insignia. She wants to recognize that long black hair, the freckles on those full brown cheeks, those eyes—fearful and happy, happy then fearful, in constant flux the way Zenaida's always were. She's thrown off by the woman's ample body, which is neither as slender or as nimble as she remembers.

Without nausea this time, she tears the name badge from her chest and whips open the door of her booth like when her cash drawer snaps out to spew a customer's change.

OCCASION

And if only I knew she'd come back;
and if only I knew what morning she'd come in
to hand me my laundered clothes, my own that
laundress of the soul. What morning she'd come in
satisfied, tawny berry of handiwork, happy
to prove that yes she does know, that yes she can
HOW COULD SHE NOT!
blue and iron all the chaoses.

— César Vallejo, *Trilce* VI (tr. Clayton Eshleman)

Zenaida ignored the metallic taste of her thirst and the nausea surging inside her, determined not to let her symptoms get the better of her. She wrapped her hand around the pencil, disregarding her employer's advice about how to position her fingers when writing.

The occasion arises and decides what occurs.

Her crooked letters stained the notebook paper like a scandal. She copied the words again on the next line, paying attention to the spelling of the original phrase written in the woman's perfect penmanship.

The occasion arises and decides what occurs.

Her apron strings came undone behind her with a tug. Isabela had been untying them lately, delighting in the repetition.

"Zena, why is your handwriting so bad?"

The girl grabbed a plastic cup and tried to slip it into her pants pocket.

"Making trouble out on the terrace, kiddo? Don't come crying to me when you get worms again."

Zenaida had heard it a few times already, the shout that reached the kitchen from the second-floor bathroom, announcing the arrival of another worm. Ever since the girl's mother was promoted at the bank and started coming home later and later, the cries had been directed at her. Isabela could feel the worms slide between her cheeks with the urgency of someone searching for light. Then they would fall angrily into the toilet and the girl would shout and flush, victorious. She imagined them being sucked through the vortex of Bogotá's sewers, passing from whirlpool to whirlpool until they reached the Magdalena River. Her mother had explained to her that all the bathroom pipes emptied out there. On a trip to the lowlands, she had shown her the river winding through the valley from above, and it had been so dazzling that Isabel could hardly believe she was looking at the final resting place of the entire sewage system. Zenaida intuited that the worms living inside the girl came from the thick shake she drank every afternoon on the balcony. She'd seen Isabela's secret ritual of mixing dirt from the geranium pot into a glass of water with a spoon she would later retrieve from under the planter. But she'd decided not to say anything to the girl's mother.

"Zena, why do you write your boyfriend so many letters?"

Into Isabela's pocket went one of the shiny spoons from the dining room table, the good ones her mother didn't let Zenaida wash with steel wool. The ones she used secretly at daybreak to eat her breakfast while everyone else was still asleep.

"Not one of those, sweetie, the dirt will scratch it all up and your mother will kill me."

She handed her a dull spoon from the drawer of ordinary cutlery meant for the two of them, sealing their complicity.

Isabela drank her dirt juice in slow gulps, with the sadness of beginning something that will end. She let the glassy pebbles scratch her molars and passed the lumps through her front teeth to break them up a bit before swallowing them. She felt that mix of horror and ecstasy she always liked to finish off with a long, deep shudder.

Zenaida went on copying her employer's neat script, which spelled out a sentence meant to help her write better. A perfect sentence for practicing the difference between *c* and *s* and *k*. A confusing sentence taken from a book. She had explained to Zenaida that it was good to get in the habit of looking up unfamiliar words in the dictionary. She had left one for her in the kitchen.

> Arise:
> \ ə-'rīz \; arose\ ə-'rōz \; ariscn\ ə-'ri-zᵊn \; arising\
>   ə-'rī-ziŋ \
> Intransitive verb
> 1a: to come into being or to attention
> 1b: to originate from a source
> 2: to get up or stand up: RISE
> 3: to move upward: ASCEND

Her spelling had gotten much better than it was when she'd started working there two years earlier. But she still confused *c*'s with *s*'s and *k*'s. Okasion. Deside. No. So when she couldn't make up her mind, she thought about Marcela's name. Marcela is with a *c* because it sounds like an *s* but comes before an *e*. As part of her spelling lessons, her boss would correct the messages she would jot down when someone called the house during the day. When Isabela spent afternoons hovering around the kitchen, keeping her company as she trimmed peas and ironed shirts, the little girl would find scraps of paper with Zenaida's clumsy handwriting crossed out in red pen by her mom. *Please call Miss Claudia at the offise,* with the right letter announcing itself on top. She would tuck them into her pocket for her collection.

"Why is it so hard to spell good?"

Isabela wanted to know why Zenaida's writing was so bad, since her mom said she had all her papers right.

"I write like this because I only got to fifth grade. But you're going to go all the way through, kiddo, so you'll be able to teach me plenty."

Zenaida once told her that her father had pulled her and her sisters out after fourth grade, saying that women who knew too much ended up on the streets. That all they'd learn in school was how to write letters to their boyfriends. What she didn't say was that when his poncho got caught in the wheel of his motorcycle, strangling him, his death had felt like a liberation. Zenaida and Nubia left Teorama to find work in Bogotá. A cousin got them jobs with decent people who paid on time and respected their days off. Marcela left home around then, supposedly for Bucaramanga, and they hadn't heard from her in a long time. When the rumor reached them that she'd joined the guerrilla, Nubia and Zenaida made a pact never to talk about her to anyone else. Their mother never said her name again. Now that Isabela had started asking so many questions about her family, Zenaida was tempted to tell her about Marcela. One day, she'd even thought of the sentence, *I have a sister I haven't seen in a long time who I think about always, and even though she's playing dead, I know she's alive.* But like the vomit that kept announcing its presence and never arrived, she'd held the words back. That was around the time the whole story had almost come out. The girl had asked what a guerrillero was and she hadn't known how to explain it.

"Someone who goes into the mountains looking for work and gets caught up in things."

Every morning, once they seized control of their respective homes and could play vallenatos full blast to rattle all the objects that surrounded but didn't belong to them, Zenaida and Nubia spoke on the phone. Temporary owners of carpets and formal place settings, they talked about the small humiliations of their days and made plans for the weekend. Sometimes they speculated about Marcela. They'd made a ritual of imagining her brave and agile in faraway wars, surviving in huts, sleeping in a hammock somewhere in the mountains.

The occasion arises and decides what occurs.

Zenaida filled the last line on the page. The wristwatch the girl had given her for Christmas said it was four o'clock. She needed to go buy milk and eggs and get dinner started before Robby came home.

"Okay, Isa, turn off the TV and come with me quick to the store."

Isabela was busy ignoring her mother's double prohibition against going into the servants' quarters and watching soap operas.

"Look, Zena, this lady's husband died and she fell in love with his twin brother because he looked just like him."

Zenaida's room was big and comfortable. But it was so close to the kitchen that it sometimes filled with smells. Back when her employer's mother used to visit, she would poke her head in and tell Zenaida to always keep her door closed. She would repeat that garlic was an aphrodisiac and terrible for a woman's health. Zenaida made Isabela eat a clove of raw garlic every time a new worm came out. To scare off the ones that were still inside.

"Come on, kiddo. Let's go look for Más."

She couldn't promise they would see the dog today. For years, Más had kept the porter of the building across the street company on every afternoon shift. But he hadn't shown up in days. The neighborhood security guard had told the children on the block that they'd taken him to a local pound where they electrocuted all the stray dogs they caught, but Zenaida tried to convince Isabela that he'd fallen in love and was just busy. Maybe he'd come back. Isabela had begun to suspect that Zenaida was lying to protect her feelings, but she still saved the hearts and wrinkled feet from the chicken stew for Más in a container in the refrigerator, awaiting his return. Some nights she cried for him, burying her face in the pillow so no one would know.

Zenaida put on a pair of jeans and unbuttoned her pale-blue maid's uniform to pull a sweater over her head. She couldn't understand how the women who worked in the other houses around the neighborhood weren't ashamed to go outside in their pastel uniforms. From the bed, Isabela fixed her eyes on the white lace bra cinched around Zenaida's back that day.

"Let me open it, Zena. Pleeease?"

Isabela had taken to standing on tiptoe and unfastening her bra through her uniform while she was cooking or doing the wash, leaving it to float under her clothes. Accustomed to these daily rituals, Zenaida responded with stoic patience, retying and refastening the knots and clasps the girl undid over and over again.

As they left the house, Isabel reached for her hand.

"Why is it so dangerous to leave the house by itself?"

"It's not anymore, not with the new grates they put on the windows. And since they fired the porter over in that building, the neighborhood is going to be safer, I think. He stole even worse than the others."

As they passed the security booth on the corner, the girl bent down to perform another ritual she had recently invented. She scooped up the chewing gum the afternoon watchman had spat onto the ground when he arrived for his shift. Having spied on him from the terrace for a long time, Isabela knew that after he put on his brown security-guard uniform and combed his hair, he would get rid of the warm, saliva-drenched bubble gum and start his workday. She took advantage of any outing to retrieve the dry, secondhand gum and soften it in her mouth.

"Isabela! What are you eating now, little piggie?"

"Gum."

Isabela concentrated all her energy on moistening the stiff purple rubber she was fervently chewing.

"It fell out of my pocket. It's grape."

"That's disgusting, Isabela. Don't pick things up from the ground like that. You know, I have a friend who ate so much junk, grass, and dirt, like you, that she got pimples all over her face. She ended up looking like an ear of corn."

Isabela considered spitting out the slimy lump, despite her almost overwhelming urge to swallow it whole. Instead, she focused on chewing it as they walked down the cobblestone street that brought them right to the supermarket.

After paying, Zenaida approached the bagger.

"I'll see you soon. Call me."

Isabela watched them angrily, dying to tell them she knew everything.

"The pimples your friend got, are they like the ones that man has?"

"No, sweetie. One day I'll tell my friend to stop by so you can see what I'm talking about. And you won't go near that junk ever again, that's for sure."

"I know stuff about you two, but I won't tell you what."

In the afternoon, after Robby got home from school, Isabela proposed making a cake. She'd decided to stop playing naked in the backyard after her brother said it was lame. Zenaida had taught her how to make marble cake, and Isabela had gotten the idea that she could sell slices around the neighborhood one day and buy her something nice.

"No, sweetie. I just cleaned the kitchen and I don't want you making a big mess in here."

Robby was singing the song Isabela hated most in the world. It always made her cry. It was a simple melody about a lonely donkey that carried his load into a thick forest in search of his master. The animal desperately wanted to find him, to make him happy. His master never appeared, and the donkey got lost in the fog and the woods.

"And no one ever, never ever, saw him agaaaaaain."

Robby held the last note for a few seconds, in the high pitch of a child just entering the sadistic phase. The donkey's bravery tormented Isabela. She'd asked Zenaida why the donkey was alone if he was so kind. Who had loaded him with fruit just to let him get lost? Why wasn't anyone waiting for him? Why didn't anyone go look for him? Zenaida hadn't been able to answer any of these questions.

"I can't hear you, I can't hear you, I can't hear you."

Zenaida had shown Isabela how to cover and uncover her ears quickly and talk in a loud voice when someone was bothering her. It was the most important piece of advice she'd ever received.

"Give me a break and don't make her cry, will you? Come on, sweetheart, come keep me company while I get dinner ready."

Isabela sat down at the kitchen table and started scratching the color off the fruits printed on the plastic tablecloth with a knife. Little by little, she forgot about her grievance. She told Zenaida that they were going away for the weekend and her mother had said she could invite a friend.

"So I'm going to tell her I decided to invite you. Want to come? There's a pool. Sayyessayyessayyes."

"I can't, sweetheart. I have plans. Why don't you invite someone from playgroup, or your cousin Karina?"

Isabela imagined Zenaida spending the weekend with the bagger from Olímpica and made herself shudder.

Her mother's car announced itself with the sound of a buzzer the girl had learned to identify. Zenaida ran out to the garage. She opened the locks, removed the chain, pushed back the bar, and swung open the gate to let her pass. From the doorway, Isabela saw her mother sitting in the car, taking longer to get out than usual. She noticed the heat coming off the motor, the fan running under the hood, the smell of cement and gasoline. She waited for her to come inside, ready to tattle on Robby for the song. She wanted to say, "Tell him, Mom, tell him he can't never sing me that song again." But her mother stayed in the car, carefully drying her eyes so her makeup wouldn't give her away. Until she finally got out and Isabela heard her heels clacking over as if nothing were wrong.

They ate in silence. Robby happily devoured the meat on his plate. Isabela put hers in her mouth, chewed it a little and pretended to swallow, then slipped it into her napkin, hoping to give it to some dog. When Zenaida cleared the table, she heard her employer on the phone, explaining the tears she'd been hiding.

"He was on the plane with the bomb. They released the list, and his name was on it."

On Tuesday, Robby told Isabela that Raimundo, that friend of their mom's who sometimes invited them to his country house where the parrots could sing love songs, had been on the airplane that blew up. Zenaida knew some of those songs too. That afternoon, Isabela helped her wax the floor, using her feet to scooch a rag across the parquet.

"Zena, have you ever had a friend die in a bomb?"

"No."

Zenaida thought about all the explosions that must have gone off around Marcela in the mountains and almost said, "Maybe."

Out on the terrace, Isabela broke up the lumps of dirt in her shake between her teeth. She looked for some sign of Más on the block, imagining him turning up suddenly on some corner, with his wise gaze and confident walk. She gulped down the final and most prized sip of her shake to run and answer the telephone.

"Zeeeenaaaa. It's some guy named Jairo for you."

"Tell him I'll be right there."

Isabela made herself shudder. She left her ear glued to the receiver the way she'd done with all of Zenaida's calls since Robby taught her how to spy without getting caught.

"How are you?"

"I'm okay. Every little thing sends me running to the bathroom. The worst is, I don't even throw up. I still haven't been able to say anything to my boss."

"But you told your sister?"

"Yes, this morning. She said I should get ready because men always split when they get this news. Promise me you won't disappear on us when the baby comes."

"My love, I've told you a thousand times. I'll do my part."

On Wednesday, Isabela kept Zenaida company while she ironed, before the others got home. They watched *Decisions: Real-Life Stories*. A woman had a baby and decided to give it up for adoption to another woman who paid her a lot of money.

"Zena, does that baby have two moms, then?"

She explained that no, only one.

On Thursday, like she almost always did when Martica came to do her mother's nails, Isabel spied on their conversation from the hallway, right beside the door. Martica's brother-in-law was also on the airplane that had blown up. She'd needed to go to identify the body on the mountain where they found the wreckage.

"People started looting right away. Pocketing rings and jewelry off the dead, going through their luggage. I got to the amphitheater and went from one black bag to another, looking at all those organs and body parts, a leg here, a piece of an arm there. I started going through the bodies that were still whole, and I found my brother-in-law. Can you imagine, a woman and some guy were trying to claim him. I mean, there were lots of people there trying to grab a piece of whatever body they could, for the insurance. And so I had to fight for mine. The woman was pulling on the body, and I had to tell her, 'No, miss, leave him alone, this body is mine so stop shaking it around.' Imagine, me not knowing my own brother-in-law after doing his nails his whole life. I know these hands, I told the lady. They'd already stolen his wedding ring. Terrible."

Isabela went to find Zenaida.

"Zena, what's an amphitheater?"

She couldn't answer the question.

That night, when Isabela called her mother in for her good-night kiss, she wanted to ask if Zenaida could sleep with her one day in the caves she made in her room with blankets and chairs. But she held back, knowing that the answer would be no.

"Mom, Zenaida is going to have a baby."

"Who told you that?"

"She told her boyfriend on the phone."

"Don't make up stories, Isabela."

"It's true. I think it was the guy from Olímpica who put the seed in her."

Isabela thought of Jairo in the red shirt of his bagger's uniform and the pin with his name spelled out on it, giving Zenaida a long, slow kiss. It grossed her out.

Zenaida came up with the glass of water she always left on her nightstand before saying good-night. Isabela looked at her belly. It was covered by the white apron she tied around her pale-blue uniform. She looked the same as always.

"See you in the morning, kiddo."

"Zena, is your baby going to live with us?"

Isabela hid under the blankets, and when she came back out, Zenaida wasn't there anymore to answer her question.

That was the first Friday Isabela didn't complain about going to spend the day at her grandmother's house. Zenaida had explained to her that repeating things and getting names mixed up was a disease old people got, that it had happened to her grandfather too. Since then, the anger she felt when she was with her grandmother, Chila, was less intense. It was wrapped in pity and fascination.

She slurped her oatmeal at breakfast, exaggerating the forbidden sounds and swooshing it around her mouth. Then she licked the milk from the bottom of the bowl to save Zenaida the trouble of washing it. For the first time, she carried her own plate to the kitchen.

"Would you like me to make you an egg?"

"No."

From the car, she watched her mother give Zenaida money and shake her hand good-bye. She remembered an episode of *Decisions* they'd watched together, where a woman got pregnant by her boyfriend but he disappeared when they called him to say she was on her way to the hospital. Gone. Because most men are like that, Zenaida had answered when she asked. And she remembered Jairo's voice on the phone. Jairo had called her *my love*. She trembled, trying to make herself shudder. She lay down across the back seat of the car and started picking off the pink polish Zenaida had painted on her nails. She covered her ears when she saw her standing at the window, saying good-bye as the car pulled out of the garage.

"Mom, why can't Zenaida's baby come live with us?"

Her mother looked at her with the stiff expression and clenched jaw that signaled the end of any conversation.

When she got home that night, she went through Zenaida's room, opening every drawer all the way, wishing she were less certain she would find them empty. There wasn't anything under the bed either. On the bare mattress, the caseless pillow still had that smell of lemon soap and firm skin that was always around Zenaida. Just like when Doreni had gone and there had been a little echo of her in the room for a week. Until her mom had made a bunch of phone calls and found Zenaida. Zenaida, the best one of all.

On the kitchen table, Zenaida's notebook and the dictionary. And a phone message taken in her clumsy handwriting, which no one had corrected. Isabela carried the notebook up to the terrace and slipped it between two planters until she figured out a better hiding place, somewhere the rain couldn't get to it. She desperately wanted one of her dirt shakes, but for the first time, she didn't let herself.

On Saturday, as she was coming back in from the terrace, her brother sang the song about the donkey, trying to make her cry. This time, she didn't cover her ears. She listened all the way through that drawn-out last word. Who was waiting for who in the forest? Would the lost donkey's journey ever end? The uncertainty disturbed her. Donkeys were so pretty, and most important, they made great friends, like dogs. Noble, Zenaida had said to her once. She hadn't heard that word before.

It was already dark, but she went back out to the terrace to drink her glass of dirt. She didn't have to hide it from anyone now. At least, not for a few days. While the occasion arose, while the new one arrived.

SAVING YOUNG LADIES

All worldly pleasures and the finest wooing
Satisfying comforts and gratifying fun;
More than elsewhere you will find this with nuns,
So quiet your mind and taste their pursuing.

-— Juan Ruiz, Archpriest of Hita, *Libro de buen amor*

The first time she saw them, Aurora felt an urgent need to save them. They were leaving the old mansion framed by her picture window in gray uniforms and white shirts. She had a burning desire to know if they faced their suffering with resignation or rebellion, and whether they really aspired to take their vows or if that was just what the nuns who presided over their hermetic three-story residence were hoping. Aurora wanted to believe that the girls martyred their fingers by biting their nails to the quick, that they chewed the erasers on their pencils down to little nubs, that they impatiently plotted the moment when they could shed the sweaters that bound their bodies and make their escape. But neither the dozen girls (or would it be more appropriate to call them young ladies?) walking down the street nor the sign out front that intoned "Saint Theresa Home for Women" satisfied the conviction of her faith.

Right after moving into the furnished apartment she'd rented in Teusaquillo, Aurora watched for the young ladies from her window throughout the day. But she only caught sight of a nun leaving the house one morning. At night she noticed a reddish glow through a second-floor curtain, which she guessed was a Sacred Heart fed by an electrical current. A flower peeked out from a pot in one of the attic windows. Madonna lilies adorned the fence around the cobblestoned front yard. The reticence of that huge English-style house only fueled her conviction that some kind of excess lay within. Aurora remembered those houses that appeared on the news in the United States, stories of women who spent years locked in a basement by sinister couples whose neighbors never caught on. She gathered later that this probably wasn't the case but sensed that her vigilance would reveal the fleeting moments when the young ladies appeared in the doorway or looked out the window, allowing her to observe just how high they pulled up their socks and what kind of frustration, apathy, or appetites were contained in their gestures. To decode their stigmata and figure out how to cure them.

Her first two weeks of surveillance bore no fruit. Until one morning the door of the residence, glass with metal grating, opened to reveal an austere entryway presided over by a statue that must have been the mystic Saint Teresa floating atop a silvery orb. From behind a decrepit nun emerged four young ladies in uniforms made of thick fabric that fell straight from their chests to their calves in a futile attempt to conceal their flesh. They wore matching scarves. Noticing the roundness budding in their bodies, Aurora concluded that they had entered that insatiable phase when girls want to gorge themselves on everything that crosses their plates. That moment of anxious appetites not satisfied by food. When she reached that age of abstract yearnings that concentrate in and cloud the body, not long after she moved to the United States with her parents, Aurora used to scrape the bottom of her yogurt cup in desperation, ashamed of her desire for so much more when it was clear there was nothing left, sensing that her distress meant something else, something wretched and essential she couldn't put into words. She pictured them anxiously sucking down every last crumb of their breakfast rolls, aware of the need to hide their zeal, to feign austerity in front of the others and the nuns. Did they buy a sickly sweet chocolate every now and then at the corner store? Perhaps they licked it slowly, enjoying a pleasure with no witnesses. Did they steal from the pantry? When no one was looking, did they wolf down leftovers in the kitchen? Aurora wanted to believe they did. She imagined them pulling back the shower curtain on those cold Bogotá mornings to give the next one her turn. She wanted to know if they looked at one another with desire. Or maybe envy tinged with desire? She sensed that the intimate choreographies of that house passed through the charged territory of the gaze.

The young ladies said good-bye to the nun who unlocked the gate for them with a boundless enthusiasm Aurora did not associate with a life of seclusion. Two of them embraced for a moment, as if to prove to the neighbors, including the one they didn't even know was watching them from above, that they still promised their friendship through touch with the easy intimacy of girls. Aurora imagined there was more to their gestures than just the remnants of childhood, that they were resisting the passage into the solitude and isolation of adulthood, the demands to which every young lady is subjected: of being a discrete body. The four of them set off down the street, pressing their books against their nipples, stoically enduring the scarves that made them sweat under the polluted sun. They brushed against one another. What reason did they have to smile so confidently? Aurora wondered if they felt pleasure as they sat on the toilet and their hot urine ran along areas rarely explored. If they were aware of it. If they preferred to ignore it.

When she wasn't walking around downtown Bogotá, Aurora spent her time at the dining room table in front of the picture window, trying to edit a novel she'd written and rewritten in the few moments she'd been able to steal from a job in New York that had just ended. She'd spent four years grudgingly

employed by a company that produced generic photos for adver-
tisements, magazines, newspapers, and billboards. She was in
charge of staging all kinds of images: a businessman holding
a globe, an ecstatic woman jumping into the air in the middle
of a crowded street, a child hugging a puppy under a hundred-
year-old tree, a white father and black mother celebrating with
their mixed-race children in a park, executives negotiating something in a top-floor office, a woman on the verge of a crisis
staring out at the horizon from her kitchen table, a little girl
pouting with boredom in a classroom, a rubber duck floating
in a real lake. She had arrived in Bogotá with what she'd managed to save during her turbulent career, one month after being
fired for sabotaging the photos by adding disturbing details to
each scene. She had the unfounded hope that she would find,
in a city she left when she was fourteen, the inspiration to finish that faded manuscript that had been gathering dust somewhere in her computer's hard drive, the only thing she had. If
she liked Bogotá, she might even look for work. Think about
staying.

But the young ladies had robbed her of the restfulness she
needed in order to face the written word. She felt like her great-
aunt, who lived near Armenia—an obsessive ornithologist who
spent her life staring at birds and wondering what emotions
they harbored about the man-made din. Meanwhile, weevils
and fungi were taking over her farmhouse, and its foundations
were beginning to rot. She was also cultivating a chronic case of
pneumonia from all the time she spent outside, searching for
birds that migrate before dusk at certain times of year. Aurora
didn't want to miss the chance to capture the exceptional movements of the elusive bodies outside her home, either. Avoiding
the carnage of the edits she needed to make to her novel, she
spent every night searching for a glimmer of disorder or discontent in the darkness of the home across the street, certain
that before long she would catch some disobedient insomniac

in a bit of mischief. But the only new detail revealed by these early weeks of spying was a room on the second floor, behind a veiled window, that had been converted into a chapel. It was lit up every evening and was most likely where the young ladies and the nuns went to finish their entreaties before going to bed.

As the weeks went by, the restfulness of the home for young ladies made the movement in the six-story building on the block behind it seem even more pronounced. Aurora noticed as soon as she moved in that the building's red balconies were always full of young men with their eyes fixed outward, like hers, regardless of the hour. A vague boredom seemed to ooze from their muscular bodies and through their tight clothes. At least, that's what Aurora thought she saw when she studied them in the light of day. An impatience they controlled by chipping away at time, an awareness that what they were hunting up there was difficult to catch and ultimately wouldn't satisfy them. When she studied them through her window, Aurora got the unsettling feeling that she was watching a television series on mute. But then the vallenatos and rancheras blasting from those balconies would reach her, and it would all begin to seem more real and concrete. And more disturbing.

One afternoon, Aurora surprised two of those adolescents (what should she call them—young gents?) surveilling the houses in the neighborhood through giant binoculars from a top-floor balcony. That is, until they reached her—probably the only one who didn't have curtains and wandered around her apartment until dawn. Aurora wagged her finger at them in an emphatic no before stepping away from the window and chiding herself for her clumsy, false courage. She'd read in the newspaper that the government had chosen her neighborhood to create "peace homes," shelters for former members of guerrilla and paramilitary groups who had decided to trade their uniforms, weapons, and military orders—given by different people, on different mountains—for a new life in the capital. Local residents complained to the mayor's office about the "throngs of demobilized fighters with nothing better to do than make trouble in our treasured historical neighborhood," as one article had put it. An explosive had gone off in front of one of these shelters a few months earlier, and the neighbors had organized to protest the lack of security. Aurora was sure that the building with the red balconies was one of those peace homes, though there was no plaque or sign to identify it. From that day on, she intensified her study of the young gents who spent their time looking for something from above, wondering about the people and animals they'd killed in their wars out in the countryside. Then she felt guilty. Wasn't it more important to welcome, embrace? Maybe that was the only thing to do in a war. So she swallowed her anger when they catcalled her from their balconies as she walked down the street. She silenced her misgivings and pretended to be a tolerant citizen. But sometimes she couldn't help herself and told them to shut up while quickening her pace.

For a short time—with the young ladies barricaded behind their walls, window grates, and curtains—the young gents, always so tangible in their porous building, quenched Aurora's thirst for spying. But Aurora grew tired of the compassion she made herself feel toward them. And that was how the young ladies, surly and elusive, won the battle. Aurora had always felt nervous bewilderment around the lucid, discerning cynicism of teenage girls. When she was that age, she'd wanted to cling to the hidden good in things, observing the world with patience and tolerance while the other girls marched resolutely toward sarcasm and unruliness. On her search for a different path, Aurora had ended up alone in her backyard with her books, unable to get to know the other girls, but fascinated by the fissures they were being drawn into. During recess they would belt out the lyrics to a popular song about soaring through a city of rage. "Me verás volar por la ciudad de la furia . . ." And then there was Aurora, who didn't know how to fly like that, but wanted to.

One week after her first glimpse of the young ladies, Aurora took advantage of a moment when four of them said good-bye to the nun who held the keys to the gate and started walking away from the old mansion to run down and meet them face-to-face. Their long hair shielded their hearts from behind. Their socks rose, tight, to their knees. They were sensuality and order. A restrained profusion. Aurora crossed the street with quick steps to catch them at the intersection where they were waiting for the light to change. The thinnest of the four, who might also have been the youngest, pulled off her sweater and tousled her hair as soon as the nun returned to her enclosure. She was saying something that held the other girls rapt.

Aurora approached them near the traffic light and interrupted their conversation.

"Hi. Do you live in that house?"

There was a collective but reticent nodding of heads.

"Nice to meet you. I'm Aurora. I live in the building across the street, on the fourth floor. I was just wondering. I moved to Bogotá a little while ago, and I'm still getting to know the neighborhood. What do you all do in there?"

The one with the tousled hair turned her head a bit to get a better look at Aurora, her eyes moving down to the boots she had on that day. She was sizing her up.

"It's a boarding school. We study with the nuns, and they prepare the ones who want to take their vows."

Her companions took a step forward, revealing the primal distrust of anything that happens in the street that is drilled into Bogotá's children from infancy. Seeing the others a few steps ahead of her, the one who'd answered hurried to join the collective sway of double-knotted shoes. As the young ladies walked away, Aurora noticed how their waists strained the seams of their uniforms. They were clearly about to discover the fascination they produced. Aurora stood in the street, watching their synchronized movements until they turned the corner and disappeared from sight. None of them turned to look at her as she'd been hoping they would. She tried to ignore the flirtatious whistles coming from the shelter. It wasn't clear whether they were meant for her or the young ladies, or for all of them. On the way back to her apartment, Aurora met the eternal, haughty gaze of the stray dog who spent mornings on her block searching for scraps and bones, carrying her nonhuman dignity on her back. Aurora always felt vaguely unsettled whenever she'd greet the animal or bring leftovers down, but she'd never wanted to figure out why.

Two days went by without anything happening in the old mansion, aside from the appearance of a few beggars who rang the bell for a plate of food that was brought to them by a cook in tight clothing ill-suited to the beatitude that reigned there. Each time the doorbell rang, a young lady would peek through the curtains of a second-floor window, but Aurora never had time to commit her face to memory. It bothered her, the silence that hung over the house, the stillness occasionally broken by the young ladies' laughter in the garage, by the sound of a ball bouncing in some internal courtyard or a body passing a window without leaving any trace. Every now and then a splotch in motion would interrupt the calm behind the glass door when they all should have been asleep. It was too fleeting. It divulged nothing.

One Thursday evening, as she went through the motions of editing her novel, Aurora saw a silhouette behind the curtain in a third-floor window that, according to her calculations, looked out from one of the bedrooms. As Aurora approached the window, the young lady pulled back the veil of the curtain to reveal the face of the one who'd been willing to speak to her days earlier at the traffic light. She raised a hand in greeting, and

Aurora returned the gesture before being overcome by shame at the thought of her bare legs, in full view of the tresses, dresses, gates, and window grates of the other. The young lady continued to stare at her, comfortable from her glassy distance, and Aurora, unsettled by her audacity, walked back to the sofa, bent her legs to hide her feet under the cushions, and grabbed a few pages, pretending to read. She looked up from her papers several times to find her still there, her forehead pressed against the window, observing her shamelessly. Until she lowered the curtain and did not let herself be seen again.

The following week, after searching in vain for the young lady from her window at different hours of the night, Aurora found an envelope with red borders and yellow hearts floating in relief in her mailbox.

Mrs. Aurora
El Zipa Apartments, 4th Floor
BY HAND

The nuns had taught them the proper way to write correspondence, maybe as a way to prepare them for a cloistered life. Maybe this was why she'd remembered to write the sender's name in neat letters.

Jessica Sofía Hinestroza (your neighbor)
Saint Theresa Home for Women
Bogotá

Dear Neighbor:
Maybe what I'm writing is the key to a safe I can't open.
I didn't get a chance to say my name the other day but I
was the one who talked to you. The others are a bunch
of uptight scaredy-cats who don't talk to anyone even me
sometimes. My name is Jessica, but here they call me Sofía

which is my middle name but the nuns say it's prettier and
it has a Christian saint. You can call me whatever you like.
To be honest, I prefer Jessica. I've been living here liter-
ally forever, like a year and eight months but it seems like
a lot more, ever since my dad died from cancer. I took care
of him until his body gave out, at least I got to be there with
him when he took his last breath. You know what? The
last book we read together was the biografy of Abraham
Lincoln but we didn't get to finish it, he's been gone almost
two years and I'm finishing it now in his honor. That's
what I was doing the night I looked for you in the window but, you know what? I don't like it really, honestly
it's kind of boring, even though the guy was so great and
famous and everything LOL. When my dad died my mom
desided to sell his hardware store and we switched neigh-
borhoods. Then it turned out she was planning to leave
for Barranquilla with some new boyfriend who was a ban-
derillero, those guys who end up all bitter because they
never made it to being real bullfighters, a total mooch.
My younger brother had no choice and had go with them
because he's so little but I said no way am I going anywhere with that guy. My aunts and uncles suggested drop-
ping me off here because this is where my older cousin
ended up of course she was here for punishment since one
day she came home with her head shaved and a tattoo and
they found some love letters she'd been writing to a friend
of hers, a girl, but she's not studying here anymore and
that's a shame because it would have been really cool to
have her for company. I did figure though that this would
be better than staying with my mom and starting over in
a new city, she's not an easy person you know. When the
nuns let us go out I always head straight for my grandma's.
We get along great thank God.
I'm not really sure why I'm writing you. I think I just
want to tell you a little bit about my life. When I saw you

the other day in the window I wanted to meet you because everyone who lives here is only nice when they feel like it. Yesterday the nun's pet who is a total suck-up called me a name while I was waiting in line for the bathroom and I wanted to rip off her towel so she'd turn bright red in front of everyone but in the end I chickened out, too bad LOL. I've realised that friends turn into enemies fast in here, or else they turn into, like, creatures that spit daggers, words that are way too sharp for a heart as cracked as mine. I'm getting tired of living with these jerks. I sometimes feel like I'm doing time in prison, paying the price for a sin I committed in another life or that someone else did.

Anyway, your probably busy so I won't bother you anymore. If you want to write to me you can give your letters to the caretaker her name is Gilma and she's a friend of mine, better if no one thinks I'm getting love letters or anything I mean I'd love to make those bullies jealous but better to keep things secret.

Okay. Bye.

Many blessings,

Jessica

She had drawn a smiley face in pink marker under her name. Aurora read the three pages again, noticing the large, heavy letters. She thought about Jessica's cracked heart. And could only imagine it as a glowing plastic decoration.

That night, Aurora waited for Jessica to appear at the window again but came to the conclusion that she'd gotten over her insomnia, which made her happy. The next day, she was about to go across the street and ring the bell, but she didn't know what to say when they opened the door, so she decided against it. The day after that, she spotted a few of the young ladies clustered around the door with guitars in their hands and rushed down to be there when they stepped outside. She was glad the nuns hadn't caught on to her fascination. They'd probably assigned all their paranoia to the men the next block over, who honed their aggressive catcalls on the young ladies.

"Behave yourselves, please. And don't be late."

The nun hurried back inside. Aurora noticed that Jessica had seen her, and she crossed the street to approach the group. Jessica broke off from the line of uniforms and waited for her as the others continued on. They exchanged greetings.

"Hey, thanks for your letter. Feel free to ring my buzzer if you ever feel like hanging out. Whenever you want. I'm in 401."

Jessica smiled a little, breaking the tension of her mouth. She looked over at the others, who had turned to wait for her. Aurora's eyes fell on the transparent hairs above her lip.

"Standing invitation. I live there alone."

Aurora wanted to smile, to see if Jessica's lips would unpurse, but she held back. She could never escape the feeling that her smile revealed a slight falseness, that it gave away how hard it was for her to live up to the benevolence it promised. She wanted to ask Jessica something mundane to soften her invitation but couldn't come up with anything in time.

"No, I mean, I can't right now. But thank you. Bye, see you soon, they're leaving me behind."

Jessica quickened her pace. The furrows of calculated indifference in her brow, her way of hiding the curiosity in her eyes behind their constant movement, her flirtation with cynicism, all announced, perhaps, her exile from childhood. Aurora wondered how easy it would have been to save her if she had still been a little girl.

The next morning Gilma rang Aurora's buzzer to give her a new letter from Jessica. It came in an envelope with a floral border. Inside was a card with a photo of two puppies begging on a heart-shaped red carpet. Their gaze was softer and less disquieting than the look the dogs that Aurora sometimes visited in the pet shops in La Caracas had in their half-closed eyes as they ignored the passers-by, their hair matted with soot from the rundown city buses. Not long before she was fired, she'd arranged the set for a similar photo of puppies on a couch, which was meant to spark feelings of tenderness and joy.

Hey nabe:
I don't know if you'll like this card. My grandma always gives me cards she buys at the stationary store, she goes there and looks through them. She doesn't have any reason to buy one or anyone to buy it for but she thinks they'll come in handy some day or maybe its to entertain herself for a little while or she thinks they'd be nice for me to have. She collects them: cards for love, humor, friendship, aniversaries, engagements . . . she even buys condolense cards sometimes even though no one died LOL. When I go visit her she sits down and shows me every single one, cracking up the whole time. I laugh with her sometimes but other times I think she's off her rocker. She always gives me my favorite as a gift, she gave me this one so I could send it to someone and I thought of you. Thanks for talking to me today, I told the others that I know you from before. I have some questions for you:
Why do you live alone, do you have a boyfriend, do you like rock music, what do you do.
Bye!
Jessica

Dear Jessica:
Thank you for the card. I saw you playing ball with the other girls in the front yard yesterday and waved to you, but I guess you didn't see me. I spend a lot of time at home so the next time you go out, just look up and you'll find me. I've been living in Bogotá for almost a month. I live alone. My parents and siblings live in the United States. I left a really boring job back there a little while ago, and I'm

looking for a new one. I decided to start fresh here, where
I was born.

I love rock music. Until recently I had a boyfriend who
played drums in a punk band, so we went out a lot. What
bands do you like? Can you recommend one from around
here?

I've been thinking of ways for you to get out of there. How
much longer do you have? What year of school are you in?
I've been thinking that if you want to leave, you can stay
here as long as you need. I have an extra room with a bed.
You could run away whenever you like. When you leave the
home with the others, for example. (About that: Where do
you go?) We could go to a rock concert or just talk.

My phone number is 245-2912, and you can call me whenever you like.

Hugs,

Aurora

Aurora reread the letter on her computer screen and decided
it would be better to copy it out by hand so it seemed less formal. She thought about adding something in the first paragraph about coming to Bogotá to finish a novel, but she worried
it might make her seem strange in Jessica's eyes. Suspicious,
even. So she didn't. In the end, she erased *run away* and wrote
leave. She took out *hugs* and put *bye,* which seemed younger,
less intimate. She considered cutting the detail about the ex-
boyfriend, which she'd invented (she was once obsessed with
a girl in her class who played guitar in a rock band), but she
decided to leave it. The letter seemed bland, but she felt as if
her mental drought, that wasteland she found herself in after
moving to a different country, wouldn't let her write anything
better than descriptive phrases. She drew a few flowers around
the edges of the page (they turned out pretty badly) and folded
the sheet into a small rectangle that she stuck to a box of rose-
shaped chocolates filled with fruit liquor that she'd bought

recently to give to Jessica if she got the chance. When she finally worked up the nerve to ring the bell at the old mansion that morning, she was slow to let go of the box as Gilma pulled it through the grating. She imagined Jessica hiding the chocolates in the section of the closet assigned to her, or under her bed. Maybe she would eat one every night, nestled under the blankets, or else she'd scurry to the third floor to wolf one down before the six o'clock Rosary. She would snap the chocolate in two with her front teeth to get at the sticky sweetness of the elixir inside. Slide her tongue into the hollow of the cracked rose. The effects of the liquor would fade quickly, but she'd feel happy and sleep peacefully. She would escape, for a moment, the frustration that radiated from her letters. Though she'd never really liked chocolates with fillings, Aurora had bought herself a box too. That way, whenever she ate one, she could imagine Jessica devouring a dripping rose in pace with her, as if by divine synchronicity.

Aurora spent several nights at the window, looking for Jessica's face behind or in front of the curtain's veil. Once she saw a body wrapped in what must have been a towel walk back and forth a few times in front of the window with the flower. She thought it was Jessica parading around, ready for her shower, and imagined her being aware that she was out there, searching for her. But her face never appeared clearly through the glass.

The following week, Aurora was just getting back to her apartment in the middle of a lightning storm when she saw Jessica and four other young ladies running toward the home. They shrieked with excitement at every thunderclap, elated the way children are by storms. They held their books over their heads to protect their hair from the ravages of the downpour. A flash of lightning made them seek refuge under the eaves of the corner store. Jessica reached Aurora's building just as another thunderclap sounded.

"It's crazy out here! You know, lightning killed a soccer player the other day right in the middle of a match, burnt him to a crisp. Stuff's no joke. Look at me, I'm soaked through."

She was out of breath. She passed the back of her hand across her face to free herself of the drops of water collecting in her lashes and then locked her eyes on the fence that surrounded her days, avoiding Aurora's gaze.

"Really? I hadn't heard."

"Yeah, a guy from Deportivo Cali, my dad's team, may he rest in peace."

Aurora drew a bit closer as if to offer the protection of her open umbrella, even though the roof was already shielding them from the rain. She reached out to catch a drop that slid down Jessica's jaw, magnifying her skin. Surprised by the invasive touch, the young lady arched away from Aurora's hand, revealing a slight tremor in her blushing cheeks, then locked her eyes on the ground. She flew off at a sprint when she saw the other girls approach the old mansion, as if set free, letting out a few excited yelps on her way to the fence where Gilma waited for them with a giant umbrella.

In the days following that inopportune touch, Aurora answered the intercom several times in the hope that she would hear Jessica's husky voice through the speaker. But it was always someone else, selling something or asking for something she couldn't give (food, money, her soul). She waited in vain for a new letter to appear in her mailbox. In the mornings, she skipped her walk downtown so she could monitor what was going on in the home. Until one day a school bus stopped out front and Aurora watched fifteen young ladies walk out carrying boxes and poster-board cutouts of sheep decorated with cotton. She figured they were the Lamb of God. (Or were they the docile flock of the Gospels? This was no time to reflect on the difference between being led as a disciple and being chosen for sacrifice.) The sincere hugs that the two nuns, convinced of their role as shepherds, doled out to each young lady as she passed through the doorway disturbed Aurora, as did her inability to imagine whom they might be off to convert. She searched for Jessica among the group and noticed that she'd cut her hair short, to her shoulders. Had she done it to look more like her? Just before getting on the bus, Jessica looked up at Aurora's window. They waved to each other. Aurora wanted to make some gesture to invite her up but couldn't, and she scolded herself for being such a coward. When all the young ladies were on board, an old nun pushed her wide body forward and ended the procession by clambering into the bus. The door closed, and they drove off. Jessica did not look for Aurora through the bus window as she would have liked.

The week after that, Aurora rang the doorbell of the boarding home with a letter asking what Jessica had thought of her proposal and inviting her again to come up and talk for a while. She suggested a system for communicating at night that involved signs they could make from their respective windows to set a day and time for their meeting, and closed with the first lines of a famous poem by Saint John of the Cross, which she assumed Jessica had learned from the nuns.

> On a dark night,
> Kindled in love with yearnings—oh, happy chance!—
> I went forth without being observed,
> My house being now at rest.

But when a small, thick nun (did they all get like that over time?) opened the door, Aurora pretended to be a representative from the neighborhood alliance coming to announce an upcoming poll about the former combatants living in peace homes. She thought about rewriting the letter without the poem but in the end decided to leave it in. The next day, after constant surveillance, she saw Gilma step into the front yard and ran downstairs to give her the envelope.

Jessica did not appear at the window any the next few evenings. At least, not during Aurora's watch, which ended when she couldn't fight off sleep anymore and gave in to the dark night.

One afternoon punctuated by sun showers, a taxi stopped in front of the old mansion. The car's horn initiated a procession of young ladies, who hurried out to collect the dozens of grocery bags that one of the nuns had brought back with her. Between comings and goings, Jessica exchanged whispers with a girl who had long, curly hair and seemed much older than her. Aurora had never seen her before. She was tall and vaguely resembled a draft horse; her thick eyebrows gave her a serious look. She exuded a sense of superiority out of sync with the breezy cheer of the others. When she tilted her head to look up at Aurora's apartment, their eyes locked. Aurora could distill nothing from that neutral gaze, which deliberately concealed inflection. So she forced herself to keep looking at the young lady, trying to mimic her tenacious indifference. They stared at one another until Jessica tugged on her companion's arm and they entered the home together.

The unsettling gaze of Jessica's confidante hobbled Aurora's obsessive investigation in the days that followed. She grudgingly returned to studying the men's building and noticed that women sometimes joined them on the balconies. The discovery bored her. She put away another letter that she'd written to Jessica, hoping she might read it inside a cave of made of her blanket. In it, she told her that she'd be at her aunt's house in Armenia for a while, to spend Christmas and New Year's there and see if she could straighten out her sleeping habits and her head. But she'd be back. Was Jessica taking a trip? To see her grandmother, or to her mother's place? If she didn't want to go back to the home, she could call her or send an email, and Aurora would go pick her up wherever she was. She closed by saying that she didn't know how many more months she'd be living in Bogotá and that they should take advantage of being so close before she left. After a few days of holding onto the letter without making up her mind to deliver it, Aurora took it to a mailing service so Jessica would receive it officially and without raising suspicion.

When she returned in January, Aurora opened her mailbox to find gas and electrical bills and an invitation to a neighborhood alliance meeting to discuss "the scourge of peace homes." Nothing from Jessica. The old mansion seemed to have shut down, as if it was on some strange kind of hiatus.

One afternoon, on the way back to her apartment, Aurora caught sight for the first time in a long while of five young ladies walking arm in arm away from the home. Jessica was intertwined with the long-haired one who had searched Aurora out from the street. Her hair had grown a bit. Her new friend was proudly packed into her sweater, her nipples aimed skyward, exercising the power of a more advanced puberty. Their whispers were interrupted by laughter as they walked toward the traffic light. Aurora picked up her pace on the other side of the street and called to Jessica. She looked over but did not respond to the hand waving at her. Then she turned back, trying to ignore the shame she felt at the greeting. Wanting to return to her former bliss, she squeezed her friend's arm a little tighter, allowing herself to be pulled along by the rhythm of her stride. They kept walking, careful not to fall out of step. Aurora hurried to cross the street and catch up to them. Jessica brought her mouth to the other's ear and said something that produced an explosion of laughter. Aurora thought of the secrets that had tormented her when she was in school, whispered by different girls more than a decade earlier. She hated that they still upset her. The young ladies turned the corner and disappeared from sight.

"Bitch! Freak!"

Aurora felt the disembodied slur was somehow directed at her. She jammed her finger trying to open the first lock on her front door, and climbed the stairs reading the water bill as if she could soften the blow of the insult with the solidity of a report in cubic centimeters. She entered her apartment and went to the window but did not see the young ladies. Her eyes landed on the shelter for former combatants, on the rooftops of other houses, and on Bogotá's mountains, soaring in their dark-green integrity, brushing against one another chaotically but appealingly. The timeless solidity of those peaks drove home the insignificance of the puny buildings that carpeted the city. The more Aurora thought about how brief her stay might be, the more she was moved by those eternal mountains. Compared to them, her presence was as fleeting as the elixir that spilled from her chocolates onto Jessica's tongue.

That Saturday, the home's white curtains were gathered on either side of its windows, revealing a table set up for iron-ing in the second-floor chapel. Aurora was excited to imagine that this was a permanent change, that some December epiph-any had led the nuns to stop hiding their labors away in dark corners and clouding the view for others. Or were the young ladies rebelling against their interference? Several of them rocked their bodies back and forth over the table, rubbing the irons in their hands across white cloth, aided by the pressure of their bellies. Uniforms and nun's habits hung from the walls. Wrapped in a towel, Aurora watched them for a while. Jessica's new friend, perhaps anticipating her future as a despot, set her iron down on the table, looked up at the fourth floor of the El Zipa Apartments, and walked over to the window. Jessica fol-lowed her, and both girls stood there staring at Aurora with the same studied neutrality. Then her friend closed the curtain with a swift, definitive movement. Aurora pulled her brand-new drapes shut and stepped away from the window. She still had so much to learn about salvation.

She figured a walk might take the edge off the feeling that she had an old refrigerator rattling shrill and off-key in her chest. That was when she saw the dog. She was with the neighborhood car washer. He'd started calling her Capricho even though she wasn't his. He knew how to respect her secrets. Every night, Capricho went out unseen, never revealing the sanctuary she found but always returning at first light. Aurora felt relieved (or was it grateful?) to see the dog every day, with her pride and her decorum, making the rounds along her block.

What if she let herself be adopted? Aurora would open her home to her. She'd give her the empty bedroom so she could spend her nights at rest, on the floor or in the bed, whatever she preferred. She'd make her soups with the fattest bones at the butcher's. She'd rub the dog's flowery breast. Battle her fleas. But not all at once, of course; she didn't want to startle her with a sudden onslaught of hospitality. She'd let her go out alone a few times every day and respect her surly, solitary nature, trusting that it would fade with time, that she would gradually forget the aged bone, the unexplored hilltop, her instinct for crossing the street. That the parasite would become a guest. She'd appeal to her nobility. And when Capricho was ready, she would take her somewhere new, inventing a pedigree for her that some gullible veterinarian would vouch for. This time, she would plan the invitation more carefully. The dog would surely be welcoming. Wasn't the guest always also a host?

In her house now at rest, Aurora turned on her computer and dragged her old novel to the trash (though the gesture seemed less definitive than throwing something in the actual garbage).

The next morning, Aurora saw a few young ladies in the front yard, sheltered in their prison of love, chatting as they weeded between the bushes, watered the lilies, and swept the dirt from the sidewalk. It troubled her, it exasperated her, that they were all so happy, that they embraced their mysteries unfazed. Jessica wasn't among them, but the other one was. So she tossed a few chicken bones into a grocery bag, grabbed a rope, and set off down the block, forcing herself to look away from the old mansion and wondering how she was going to convince Capricho, so peaceful in her lucid and joyful solitude, that there was no better idea than being saved.

FAUNA OF THE AGES

> *But how is our story of love to be*
> *if I am food to you, and you the eater of me?*
>
> — A mouse to a crow, *Kalila and Dimna*

SEPTEMBER 22, 2004

My days are a waking nightmare. My nights, too, I guess. Maybe it's a question of numbers. The whole thing is because of a bunch of fleas that ended up sucking on my legs when the cat whose fur they used to live in moved out with its owner and I rented her apartment. Their offensive has been unrelenting. Last week I counted forty-eight bites on my body. This week the number went down because I've declared insecticide war on the little buggers. I imagine this drove a few to jump from my balcony in search of other lodgings.

The struggle has given me an intense nervous tic. I imagine I'm being bitten every ten seconds and slap various parts of my body hard, hoping to squash one in the act. But I never know if it's really them or not. Estefanía once said that Bogotá is a special city because every time you go to the movies you get bitten by a flea. She applauded this form of solidarity, which can't be found in most first-world latitudes. But I doubt that the new movie theaters thundering in shopping malls today, with their antimicrobial seats made of imported plush, are particularly appealing to fleas. My mother, who described the bubonic plague in detail to us when we were very young, added a scientific fact to the discussion: fleas prefer women to men.

I want to test this theory, if I don't die first like a martyr full of itchy stigmata and dangling scabs, with irritated eyes that see potential bloodsuckers in every speck or fleck floating around.

OCTOBER 11, 2004

Last night, as I touched a body free of welts, I looked over the man's shoulder and saw a tiny black dot standing out against the white weave of the comforter. A flea, I thought, as my coexistence with those gluttons had trained me to do. I interrupted my hand's journey along its sinewy path to touch the dot, convinced that a flea couldn't possibly just be sitting there, relaxed, watching us roll around in bed. I touched it and it gave a little hop, as if it didn't want to lose its view of the giants in front of it. A flea! I shouted as the man sighed. I grabbed it as hard as I could between my thumb and forefinger and got up, abandoning the naked man, and set about slowly drowning it under the bathroom faucet, making sure that it slid down the slimy, wet pipes on its way to a distant septic fate. I wanted the drain to feel like a terrifying void. I wanted that pest to weep and let out little panicked cries as it plummeted downward. I wanted it to vanish forever from the land of the living. You ruined my night, vile flea, I said and returned to bed with a weary sigh. K. told me that he hoped I wouldn't act the way I did when a protozoan set up shop in my intestines on my trip to Peru, then turned to face the wall. I fell asleep.

DECEMBER 9, 2004

The fleas' return to my life has been gradual but efficient. Last week I found two bites on my ankle, right next to one another, as if the flea had sucked a little blood, walked the width of a few hairs, and realized it needed some more before its nap. Like when you fill up on delicious pork rinds but reach for another, anyway. I ignored these bites so I didn't have to think about September's fleas. But today, as I put on the blue robe I read in, like the unemployed woman I am (it's a shame I'm not more busty or bigger around the ass and hips to fill out my fantasy of matronhood, and that the only one who watches me through my window is the ailing rooster in my neighbor's yard), I discovered a monumental welt on my left leg. I think they're coming back, little by little, to torture me. The return of the repressed, motivated by hemoglobin. Less metaphysical, more carnal. What am I going to do to run them off?

DECEMBER 10, 2004

The flea banquet continues. Today I counted nineteen bites: crease of the knee, elbow, other hidden corners. K. said to me, "I think you're pregnant and the father's a flea." Definitely possible.

DECEMBER 17, 2004

Inventory (flea bites over the past three days)

BODY PART	BITES	ITCH	OBSERVATIONS
Feet and ankles	10	Under control	They prefer the left.
Legs	56	Brutal	They prefer the left.
Buttocks	1	None	Has scabbed.
Belly	2	Waning	. . .
Breast (left)	9	Getting worse	Burning sensation.
Back	10	Under control	Might be more.
Arms	15	Awful at night	They're so skinny, what's the appeal?

DECEMBER 21, 2004

Bouquets of white rue fill my room. My mattress smells like eucalyptus, and I do, too, because I douse myself (especially my boobs) with the oil every night. I'm battling the fleas on olfactory terrain. But I know that the slightest lapse could rouse them again. I leave for a while, hoping they'll die of starvation once and for all, or that in a final act of desperation they'll line up to jump from my balcony in a mass suicide.

JANUARY 6, 2005

They must have taken advantage of my absence to reproduce. Strict adherence to my embargo of movie theaters was clearly not enough. The last time I went to see a film in Teusaquillo I was scratching for weeks. How many movies have I missed? But now I'm waking up again with bites behind my knees, their favorite spot to feast on. And one right next to the fold of my breast. I submit my body to another observation period to see if more appear. My experience with them has been so transformative that now, when I walk around downtown and fantasize about leaving the country and coming back with money, or moving to a new spot and having some plants to call my own—whenever my mind drifts in that direction, I shudder to think about having to wage a grisly war on fleas in my future new home. And so my plans crumble and I stop thinking about tomorrow.

JANUARY 7, 2005

Gustavo confessed to me over chat today that he's part of the conspiracy.

G:

this is a wurning: if u dont pey the rensom we wil haf to proseed with the exacushun of ur frend k. sined: the kiler fleas

ME:

But I spent all my money on pesticide!
Have mercy!

G:

no mersi
fleas haf human rites to
o and one mor thing
u mite want to change ur diet ur blud is kinda bland

ME:

but you bit my knees just last night and eight times on one arm
that's proof that you like my blood
and besides i've been eating a lot of chocolate lately

G:
theres jus nothing beter arownd

ME:
oh
well go bite someone else then
there's a dog and a fat eight-year-old downstairs from me

G:
yuk! wut do u tak us for?

ME:
there are other women in the building

G:
but ur thc tastycst

ME:
No! Have mercy

G:
tonite
we wil karry out a komando operashun

ME:
Oh no
please, no!

G:
we r going to kil u

ME:
noooooo pretty please

G:
luv u to peeces

ME:
listen there are dogs who need me
and i'm not interested in your kind of love

G:

ooooooooooo
u made us cri
we get it
okay then its bin a pleshur
we fleas haf our pride to

ME:

good
Take your pride for a long walk off a short pier and leave me
alone

G:

fine ofer ur flesh to other bists see if we kare

ME:

I already have
And it's much more pleasant
than the itch from your kind of love

G:

u wont heer from us agen
u mak us cri

ME:

do you cry tears of blood?

G:

bitursweet and angwished

JANUARY 20, 2005

While my battle against the hatchlings that managed to sur-
vive my absence rages on, new animal company arrives. This
time, though, I welcome it. According to my childhood super-
stitions, the spiders visiting my home bring good luck. I greet
them from a distance using the soft voice of someone talking
to a puppy and desperately hope they'll stay a long time. One
visited me in the shower a few days ago, but in the morning

I found it dead next to the shampoo and worried it might be a bad omen. Today another one came to visit me next to my comb (what a lucky woman I am, I thought in a moment of egomania), and I tried to save it from the cleaning lady. Explaining the situation, I pushed it gently away from the sink toward the corner where I hoped the woman wouldn't see it and squish it beneath her antibacterial iron fist. She's in there now, I can hear the *plaf plaf* of her rag, and I wonder if the spider managed to camouflage itself or curl up in a little ball, if it was able to protect itself from the bleach and scrub brush, guaranteeing me all the luck that the one who drowned in the shower, may she rest in peace, could not.

FEBRUARY 16, 2005

A ruthless fumigation brought an end to the infestation a couple of weeks ago (to the delight of my lacerated flesh). But then yesterday a cockroach with spots like a leopard appeared in my desk drawer. It had apparently been living there among the photocopies and receipts. And the fleas. With eternal calm, K. picked it up and tossed it out the window so it could invade the apartment on the first floor (I guess it's not so bad if it helps them out with their food a little, everyone in that place is morbidly obese). There's only one flea left (at least, I hope so). It's expiring on the parquet floor and I let it move its legs slowly, wanting to witness the end of its bloodline in real time. You're just like your ancestors, horrid flea. That's something my mother taught me when I was very little: we could all still die from the bubonic plague.

FEBRUARY 17, 2005

I sit down to fill out a tax form, and when the bureaucrats ask me, "Do you have children or other dependents?" I get flustered because there's no space there to explain that I feed fleas, cockroaches, spiders, neurochemical deficiencies, and Other. And that all this should qualify me for an exemption.

MARCH 1, 2005

All signs of the bites are gone. In order to avoid future infestations, I'm thinking of catching the libertine cat that makes his rounds atop the walls in the neighborhood and always eyes the neighbor's rooster with a touch of rage. Does he belong to someone? Fleas like the warm nooks and crannies of other animals even more than they like women. The cat would save me from new batches of fleas; he'd be the one to adopt them as dependents. And I'm sure he'd bear the whole thing with more dignity. I'd take good care of him, make him beef broth and lavish him with attention, and the circle of dependencies that captivate and hold us all would begin to close.

COLLATERAL BEAUTY

So I'm left to pick up
the hints, the little symbols
of your devotion.

— Antony and the Johnsons, "Fistful of Love"

"Keep an eye out for unexpected opportunities." That was the horoscope's prediction for Estefanía one August Saturday as she waited in the empty clinic. There was an article in the same magazine titled "The Universe Is Slowly Dying," which seemed both obvious and unsettling, so she refused to read it. As she sat behind the counter, sticking a fat needle she'd found in the drawer of scalpels and suturing instruments into the raised skin of a blister on her foot, Estefanía wondered if the message, the one about opportunities, foretold her trip to New York. Could be, though she'd always distrusted horoscopes as an act of rebellion against her mother, who was obsessed with magazine astrology. As she put her shoe back on, she immediately regretted getting carried away by the clear morning and leaving the house without socks. After completing the operation, she passed a rag across the counter, a glass display case that housed tiny shoes, hats, and other doll accessories, together with stuffed animals that had recently come out of surgery and were waiting in plastic bags to be claimed by their owners. It was almost always girls and women who came into the clinic, and their visits were getting less frequent.

She pulled the six antique dolls from their bags, getting them ready for the elegant old woman who had hospitalized them earlier that week, requesting different surgeries for each. Even naked, they exuded a dignity sculpted by the decades; even without their starched dresses made of dupioni, lamé, and lace, without the velvet or linen shoes they arrived in, they bore their seams and joints with relative vitality and pride.

"I've invited my friends to a special tea. They're going to bring their childhood dolls. They've nearly all saved and preserved them. Since we're all so old now, it's going to be an antique show."

That's what the woman had said to her as she unpacked the box of injured dolls. Estefanía imagined a banquet of well-coiffed and heavily perfumed women, expanding their spongy flesh with succulent pastries in a grand dining room while the eternal girls with their firm little bodies avoided their gazes from tiny chairs. Maybe each woman would tell the story of her doll, the details of how it came into her life and how long her faith had lasted—how long she'd believed her doll had a soul. Maybe the pitch and rhythm of the women's speech would change when they talked about them, and the green of their childhood voices would break through the parch of their old throats for a moment. And there the dolls would sit, indifferent to their reveries.

"You have a treasure here, ma'am. And I know about these things, I grew up in this clinic and I've seen it all."

In the thick intake book, an archive of the past fifteen years of doll diagnoses and treatments, Estefanía wrote down symptoms as the woman described them to her. Her handwriting seemed clumsy and profane beside the neat letters of her grandfather and her mother, who had been in charge of the registry before her.

"Leonor, who belonged to my cousin Leonor, needs to have her face redone because her eyes and lips have faded. I do store them carefully, you know, hidden away so no one touches them.

Under my bed, wrapped in tissue paper. Beatriz, this one with the jet-black hair, her arm is loose. She might need to have her rubber replaced where it's torn. Ingrid, well, she's not as old as the others, but she belonged to my daughter's German friend. I made the mistake of giving her to my granddaughters for a little while, and look at her hair now, all uneven because they got it in their heads to cut it, just look at this mess. Awful. She'll need a hair transplant. And please, something of quality."

"Don't worry, I have the perfect thing. We have a bit of the hair my grandfather imported from France years ago, when they still made it. It's a pretty color, light just like this."

"Perfect. I'd like it long, to her shoulders. Don't worry about the cost, as long as it goes with her skin tone. And María Inés, look at this beauty, she's from England, turn of the century, look at this little hook she has in her back, just look, she nods yes or no when you pull it. Look, look, she's saying 'No, no, no!'"

Estefanía imitated the woman's peal of laughter. It had been a long time since she'd been able to laugh like that, about those prosaic things that make people howl as if there were some unforgettable joke hidden under the surface.

"Isn't she divine? This finger is broken, it needs to be plastered and refinished. Her nails should be repainted too. And look at Shirley Temple. My father gave her to me back when we lived in England and went to see her in a movie, one of the first ones she did as a little girl. Of course, how would you know anything about Shirley Temple? She was a child actress, a big movie star in the thirties. Adorable, with golden curls just like this one here. When she became famous they made dolls of her. They were all the rage. I'll never forget the day I opened the white box she came in. I was so excited I almost died. This one is a real collector's item. She needs to have her leg fixed, it started turning the wrong way. I'll bet it was the girls, they must have taken her out of the box without permission."

The old woman grabbed the doll's leg and forced it back to center.

"And this Arabian doll, or, well, I'm not sure if she's Gypsy or Arab, but she's a gem, just look how fine she is. She's from France. She belonged to my friend Lucia, who lived in Vienna for a while. She was meant to have some strange name, Lucia told it to me on her deathbed, but it was impossible to remember so I baptized her Lucy. She told me she returned from Europe by ship, and when she reached the Magdalena River, she stood on deck with the doll in her arms so she could see the whole view. This was back when the Magdalena was a different river, a real beauty. Before it turned into a shallow sewer. So as you can imagine, Lucy has seen it all. The Seine's cupolas and the monkeys and deer along the Madgalena. An absolute gem. You'll need to fix her toes, too, they're all cracked. And to straighten this eye, it wanders to the side."

Estefanía had promised to have them all fixed up by Saturday at noon so they could attend their tea that Monday.

"I'm so glad I finally managed to come in. I've been passing by this place for more than a year and thinking I absolutely needed to, but I'm only just getting around to it. I finally made it out to take care of my friends. I call them that, you see, my friends, because just imagine how long we've lived together. I saved more than a few of these friends from the ones with flesh and bones who had no idea what to do with them and nearly left them to the maids."

As she waited for the owner of the most distinguished specimens to have passed through the Reyes Family Doll Clinic since Barbie and other products made in China flooded the market, Estefanía imagined being the housekeeper of a woman like Doña Cecilia. She'd have a light-blue uniform and a starched apron and might feel embarrassed about wearing them out in the street. She would spy on the meals served in the fine lady's dining room through a little window in the kitchen door. When the leftovers from the afternoon tea came back in, decimated, she'd polish them off. Maybe she'd even sneak a pastry or two before they made their way to the grand table. Then she tried to imagine, but could not, what it would be like to have that job in New York, where an upper-class woman like Cecilia would have more money and who knows what customs. Maybe the same ones. She remembered the horoscope she'd read earlier. It might have been predicting an imminent trip to New York. Maybe it was foretelling the arrival of a buyer for the clinic's storefront. Or that she would get her visa. She wanted to believe that all this radiated from the faint lettering of a magazine horoscope.

Estefanía had promised her cousin Shirley they would spend that Halloween together in New York. She'd said it less out of conviction than desire. It would be their first Halloween together since Shirley moved there two years ago, after finally receiving the green card her father had applied for a decade earlier. Estefanía had announced that she'd already figured out her costume for the party. She was going to be a stray dog. She'd wear her hair all dirty and tease knots into her curls so it looked matted.

"I'm going to hang a sign that says 'Hi, I'm a stray dog' around my neck."

Shirley had told her that there weren't any stray dogs in New York. That no one would understand her costume. That she would have to explain too much, and that people would think she was crazy. That she should pick something less depressing.

"Hi, Aunt Martica. I opened the clinic early today because there's a customer coming to pick up an order. It's the craziest thing, I forgot to tell you, a collection of antique dolls. A real treasure. My grandfather would have died of excitement to see them restored. So yeah, I close up at noon today. I'd be happy to go with you if you come get me. I can't wait to see your new look."

Her Aunt Martica, Shirley's mother, promised to pick Estefanía up on her way back from the prison where she was visiting her most pampered client, a businesswoman who had been caught storing supplies for processing cocaine in one of her warehouses. Martica was manicurist and masseuse to a long list of clients she'd built over years of hard work. She specialized in nails, firming and slimming massages, serums, and secrets. After countless massages and many years spent developing strong arms and a soft body to cushion the hands and feet of others, Martica had managed to ascend to the ranks of the triumphant middle class. She did so well that she was able to pay for Estefanía's high school after her mother died, and had promised to help her pay for a trip to New York to study English now that she'd graduated. With Shirley there and her aunt's offer, Estefanía nurtured the hope of going, at least for a while.

That afternoon, Martica was going to show Estefanía her new face. Her return to some kind of youth. The plastic surgeon who sent her clients to Martica for post-liposuction massage therapy had given her a new face for her birthday a few weeks earlier. Instead of the free facelift that she had originally been promised, Martica had received an even bigger gift as she slept peacefully under anesthesia. The doctor had sculpted her a slimmer face with a pointier nose, higher cheekbones, and a smoother jawline. A welcome face, but not the one she'd requested. After two weeks of recovery, Martica still had a few bandages wrapped around her head, but the swelling had gone down almost completely. She wanted Estefanía to be one of the first to see her, now that she was ready to reenter the world.

When she'd finished the magazine with her horoscope, Estefanía opened her grandfather's copy of *Don Quixote*, which always sat right next to the accounting books on the shelf. She had decided to read it the week after she graduated high school, but skipping around, picking chapters at random. When she was little, her grandfather used to tell her what was happening in the chapter he was reading on those Saturdays she spent with him at the clinic. She opened to one titled "Concerning what befell Don Quixote on his way to Barcelona" and wanted to believe that it was another sign of her impending voyage to unknown lands. When the phone rang again, she figured it had to be the woman with the dolls letting her know that she couldn't make it in. After all, she was about to close. But instead she was met with the deep, halting voice of a man with a strange accent asking for the Reyes Family Doll Clinic. He explained that he was calling from the United States. That he was employed by Saint Ignatius of Antioch Church in New York, and that he'd found the clinic's information online after a friend from Colombia recommended it to him.

"I'm looking to buy figurine parts and antique dolls for our altar."

Estefanía tried to adopt a secretarial tone. She explained that the clinic only repaired children's dolls and stuffed animals. She could get him the number of one of the antique shops in the neighborhood, though.

"You see, what I'm really looking for is colonial saints, but that's not all I'm interested in. I'm also looking to buy all sorts of antique dolls, as well as parts and pieces. Perhaps you could help us find some."

He promised generous compensation. Estefanía told him she probably had a few things that would interest him. She had to look. She wrote down his email address so she could send him a list and photos of the items. Antonio Pesoa had an Argentinean accent and the voice of an ascetic hermit speaking for the first time in ages, from the confines of a small cave.

Before wondering whether the call might be a prank, Estefanía thought of the money the deal would bring in. Of the chance to finally get rid of the inheritance of limbs, eyes, and hair that her grandfather had left to her mother, and her mother had left to her and her brother. Juvenal had already been informed of the clinic's impending closure, and Martica was trying to find him another job. Someone would buy the storefront sooner or later. And if she got her visa, she'd finally make the trip to New York. She'd go see Shirley and sign up for the English course she'd found in Queens. She'd learn the language. She'd stay in New York for good and eagerly await Martica's visits twice a year. She would start to believe in horoscopes.

In the back of the shop, a teddy bear, a doll with a chewed nose, and a legless Barbie with red hair awaited Juvenal's intervention. After a brief but intense struggle, Estefanía opened the door to the small storage area on the far side of the room for the first time since her mother's death. The drawers of the dresser to her left were marked *Porcelain Parts, Clothing, Face, Religious,* and *Shoes* in her grandfather's neat hand. On the other side of the room was an old counter piled with arms, legs, torsos, and shopping bags full of blond heads, as well as heads for teddy bears and stuffed dogs, hands, and plastic hips labeled *flesh-colored,* a euphemism for the shade of white that all the dolls coddled by the little girls of Bogotá were painted. Several rolls of fabric and one of synthetic fur gave off a smell of mothballs in one corner.

"Neither of them ever threw anything away."

With the first arm Estefanía lifted from the pile of amputated surplus, a large eye fell out and rolled across the red tiles toward a corner of the little room. When she bent down to grab it, she noticed the green and black stripes of its irises. The glass had cracked a little bit, but only in the back, so the fissure wouldn't show when it was set in a doll's head again. Estefanía recognized the old technique of painting on glass. They didn't make them like that anymore. These days, eyes weren't three-dimensional or removable, they were just drawn onto the plastic, depriving the dolls of the freedom of peripheral vision and the ability to look nervously this way or that to meet or evade the gaze of their owners. Children are spoiled by the eyes they do today, she thought. They promised the security of a gaze always there waiting for them and taught them to expect they would always be special. That's why she was never going to have kids. Even that eye of yesteryear might bring her good money in New York. She stuck it in her pocket on her way to see what the dresser held.

In a drawer marked *Antiques* she found three dolls wrapped in tissue paper, which she removed carefully. There was a gypsum doll the length of her forearm, with black hair, a round face, a mouth pursed in the shape of an *o*, pale pink cheeks, and flawless skin, bundled up in a shawl and matching dress. She looked like a stout woman from a town in the Andes ready to set up a stand in the market square, but the tag hanging from her wrist read *Germany, 1870*. The next one she unwrapped was naked. Its pubic area was made of rough canvas, its public areas of the finest porcelain. A pair of legs that turned into porcelain at the knee and ended in black high heels hung loosely from its soft torso, in danger of coming unstitched. The doll's arms were in good shape, with the exception of a crack in the palm of one hand and half a finger that had broken off. Its lips were pursed on the verge of a pout, and a few teeth could be seen in the space between them. It had blue eyes and long lashes, and dark hair painted on to just below the ears, as was the style. *France, 1918*. Despite her flagrant nudity and the anonymity of decades spent in a dark drawer, there was nothing sinister about her. She seemed headstrong but also polite. From a small box Estefanía removed an androgynous baby in lace swaddling that even encircled its head, forming a kind of crown. The head was the only notable part of the body. *Bisque porcelain,* read the tag written in her grandfather's hand. Sheathed in lace, the doll's face was dominated by two enormous gray eyes, shiny and open wide, surrounded by long lashes that heralded a future of intense grief. *Vienna, 1901*. It begged to be taken out for a stroll by a nanny, around a city from a different era. It could certainly play the baby Jesus in a Manhattan church at Christmastime.

Other items from her grandfather's collection of antique remains appeared in the list Estefanía sent to the strange Argentinean who had called that morning.

- Black infant in bisque porcelain, crack in one leg and small hole in one heel. Rubber intact. Missing head. Chubby. Tag reads *France, 1926.*
- Assorted parts: one pair of eyes, painted wood with inlaid glass irises and pupils. Four pairs of glass eyes in different colors. Single eye, lightly scratched on the back. One pair of porcelain arms attached to cloth. One pair of medium wooden feet. One pair of plaster feet (5 cm long).
- Other: miniature perfume bottle in blue glass; embroidered knit socks for a large doll; small ivory fan with floral design; white leather gloves with black embroidery; small metal mirror; leather-bound doll's diary, can be opened; porcelain lapdog with brown fur and an open mouth that reveals a painted tongue inside.

"Come take a look, sweetheart, and tell me what you think."

From inside the storage room Estefanía heard Martica's voice and went out to meet her.

"Gorgeous!"

"Sometimes I think this royal face doesn't go too well with the body I've got."

"You look great, Aunt Martica."

"The swelling still needs to go down a bit more before I look like one of those fancy dolls you said someone left here."

As she climbed into Martica's car, Estefanía noticed something in her pants pocket digging into her leg. It was the glass eye she'd forgotten to leave in the pile of old figurines when she ran out to see the other doll in her life.

Estefanía spent the next week waiting for the woman to reclaim her dolls. A few orders came in, which she received with great efficiency and which kept Juvenal busy for a while: a teddy bear that vomited fill from a tear in its shoulder, three bland little dolls who had ended up in a child's beauty parlor and couldn't pull off their new punk hairstyles, and one of those dolls that pee, which needed a new torso because its owner had poured drain solvent down the tube that ran from its mouth to its groin. But the date of the tea had come and gone, and the elegant dolls remained behind the counter. Inclined to tragic thoughts, Estefanía imagined their owner in a casket, seized by a rigor mortis of longing.

On Friday, she decided to call the number the woman had left on the receipt. A housekeeper informed her that Doña Cecilia would be traveling for an unspecified period. When Estefanía explained that the clinic would be closing soon, for good, and asked what she should do with the dolls, the woman disclosed that her employer had been in a nursing home since the weekend before, that her son had returned from abroad to take her there. The housekeeper offered to ask about the dolls and promised to have an answer for her the following week.

Estefanía looked through the glass counter at the dolls' faces, all wrapped in plastic, and knew she needed to save them. They didn't deserve to be in that chipped display case for one moment longer.

Estefanía:
Your message has given us immense pleasure. We wish to purchase all the items you offer. Though some of the objects you mention do not fall under the rubric of religion, they will suffice just the same. We can offer you three hundred dollars for the lot. Should you be interested, we would need to determine a means of shipping the items to New York. I'll look into different parcel delivery services this week and follow up with you. I wish I could travel to Bogotá to pick them up, but that is a fantasy. I await your reply.
Antonio Pesoa

Dear Estefanía:
I forgot to ask you in my last email if by any chance you have a ventriloquist's dummy among the items available for purchase. Please say you do! Let me know as soon as you can.
A.

Having called the number left by Doña Cecilia for two weeks with no response, Estefanía decided it was time to find asylum for the exiled dolls. She'd searched for the woman's address so she could bring them to her home, but it wasn't listed in the phone book. Maybe she had told her the story of each one in so much detail because she was leaving them to her. Maybe she cried out for them in the drugged stupor of afternoons in the psychiatric ward and everyone thought the names were yet another symptom of her malady.

After another two weeks of waiting and several failed calls, Estefanía accepted the dolls as her irrefutable inheritance. That night she dreamed of the six of them adorning a gilded colonial altar. In each section of the altar was a doll wearing a starched saint's gown and tunic, with a rosary dangling from hands recently repaired by Juvenal. Antonio entered, dressed all in black with a woolen cap covering his bald head. He seemed to be floating, as if he was being pulled by a string from his belly. He knelt at the first pew. Estefanía stepped inside the church and tried to approach the altar, but a furious priest threw her out in unintelligible English. Antonio said nothing; he just looked at her, deeply moved. Estefanía stood in the doorway, sobbing next to a leper reeking of urine who begged for alms, and realized she was in the Church of Saint Frances in downtown Bogotá, where her grandfather used to take her when she was a little girl.

Dear Estefanía:
It would be wonderful if you sent everything with your aunt next week. It would have to be packed well so none

of the little pieces break, given how delicate they are already.
The loose eyes! Yes, we want them, absolutely. And we're
just thrilled about the other dolls. We could pay you four
hundred dollars for them, if that figure seems fair to you.
They must be strange treasures, indeed. But of course,
things worth treasuring tend to be strange. They're the
ferment that escapes the mold.
I like your idea of decorating an altar with these alluring
dolls.
Make sure they shine according to their essence.
I'm dying to get my hands on a ventriloquist's dummy
from the colonial period. They're very hard to find. I want
to propose a kind of religious-didactic performance to
the other priests, between a ventriloquist (dressed up as a
saint or a virgin) and his doll (which could play the role of
angel or a soul, or something like that).
I can pick up the delivery and pay your aunt directly, as you
mentioned. My phone number, so she can call me when
she gets to New York, is (212) 945-3850.
Please write back and tell me more.
Warmly, A.
P.S. Thank you for sharing your dream with me. In my
version, were my dreams to shimmer, I would attack the
priest, tie him to the column, and force him to perform
hara-kiri, then I'd take you to see the newly canonized dolls
and the ventriloquist playing a soul in purgatory. But don't
take me seriously. I haven't slept in days.

A fine rain misted the city on the September morning when
Estefanía took Doña Cecilia's dolls out of the counter display
and carried them over to one of the long surgical tables. Juvenal
was working at the other one, sewing a new pair of ears onto an
enormous Saint Bernard. One by one, the dolls allowed themselves to be laid flat. Their naked bodies revealed their new precarity. Estefanía walked over to the storage room, opened the

drawer marked *Clothing,* and pulled out a bundle of dresses wrapped in tissue paper. Leonor looked pretty in a blue satin dress with a petticoat. The lace tunic worked for little Beatrice. The pleated dress with short sleeves was good on Ingrid, topped off with a simple white coat. And so on. She found something to cover each of them, so they wouldn't have to travel in just their inner majesty. Antonio would need to find them more suitable dresses for the altar. She pulled a few small rosaries made of orange and rosewood from the drawer of religious objects and put one on the arm of each doll. She packaged them one by one in bubble wrap and laid them in the boxes she'd gotten for their journey. Then she dusted off the dolls in the storage room and the body parts she'd promised Antonio, resting each one on a bed of foam scraps and paper shreds.

The sun was just rising in Bogotá when Estefanía went to the airport with Martica. Martica made the trip to New York when the big department stores had their sales. She traveled light and came back with two suitcases full of clothing her clients in Bogotá had ordered, which she sold to them with a commission that covered her expenses and padded her savings account. She used to stay with her sister, the one who worked at a factory in New Jersey assembling tiny pieces of airplane motors, but ever since Shirley moved to New York, Martica has been staying in her daughter's apartment.

The two boxes with the dolls and other objects for Antonio were selected for inspection by the antinarcotics unit as Martica waited in the long line to check in at the airport. One police officer had a young dog that wagged its tail furiously as it searched the boxes for cocaine. The officers urged it on, trying to get it to find the valuable powder, but the dog showed no interest. Confirming one last time that the shipment contained no illicit substances, one of the police officers took out the Arabian doll, unwrapped it, licked his index finger, ran it along the doll's leg, and returned it to his mouth. When he didn't taste the alkaloid he expected to find diluted in its skin, he gave the final order to close the boxes. A few days later, Martica called Estefanía to say that she'd delivered the boxes to Antonio and had the money in hand.

"All he said was thank you, ma'am, and added that I have a lovely niece. He also said he wants to meet you, sweetheart."

Crowned, victorious one:
(That's the etymology of your name, did you know?) I received the beauties you sent, despite the mishaps. If I were an airport police officer, I would have confiscated them all without the help of any dog and made a run for it. You can rest easy, your grandfather's treasures will be venerated here. The doll that moves her head to say *yes* and *no* arrived with an injured hand. Could she be the one the dog sniffed? Perhaps the gesture rattled her humors.
I thought about her yesterday, and also about you, and about matters of the flesh, because I almost took a little old lady's finger off at the gym. I was using one of those weight machines; she stuck her hand in, and I smashed her finger. We had to call an ambulance. It was absolutely pulverized. She'd stuck it right between the weights. There was blood everywhere, which wasn't entirely a bad thing because it snapped all those people staring at themselves in the mirror back to reality a bit. The ambulance arrived forty minutes later and no one got out so I went to see what was going on, and the girl behind the wheel was busy putting on lipstick. Anyway, the eternal mysteries of athletic life. Good Lord. The old lady was quite stoic, thank goodness. But who puts their hand right where weights are going up and down? I told her I was sorry and that I'll never go back there. And to think, I'd managed to drag myself to the gym for a couple of weeks straight. I blame it all on one of those guys who sells exercise equipment on television. This one has a disgusting blob of resin that he

claims is pure fat, and he calls it "Mr. Fat" and goes on and on about how it lives inside you. Have you seen him? I was so disgusted that I paid for a year-long gym membership in advance. But I can't go back after the incident with the old lady. I'd rather be here, in my cave, caring for my injured doll.

Your aunt said you might visit New York soon. When you do, I'll take you out for tea and we'll have some delicious pastries filled with peaches from a distant island in the Japanese archipelago. And talk about any old thing.

I'll send you photos soon of these contemplative girls in their new home.

Write to me. About whatever you like, anything will do. Of late, my nights consist of trying to keep my thoughts at bay—they're like search dogs with a deafening bark.

Thank you, your majesty.

Warmly, A.

Estefanía reread the message. She wished it had been written by hand. Her aunt had told her that Antonio was extremely shy, one of those men whose silences reveal more than what the rest of us know. Estefanía thought of a wild horse running across the plains of Asia, of those four-thousand-year-old pines that still grow on the hills of the Middle East. Antonio must be something like that.

The liquidation of the Reyes Family Doll Clinic lasted four weeks. The space sold quickly and for a good profit. A developer was buying up the whole block to build luxury apartment buildings like the ones going up all over Chapinero. Juvenal decided to drive a relative's taxi while he waited for a job with one of Martica's clients to come through. Estefanía took the things she wanted to save: a couple of paintings of European dolls sitting in chairs in a park in spring, which her mother had hung in the operating room; the collection of miniature hats for sale in the counter display; the business's sign and accounting books; dolls that were left over after the liquidation; *Don Quixote*. Some pieces of furniture and other remnants were donated to a school for the blind a few blocks away. The rest went to the garbage pickers. When Estefanía locked up for the last time before turning the shop over to its new owners, it occurred to her that one day she'd come back from New York and not recognize the dirty, rundown corner of her childhood, and she would feel an emptiness.

In the airplane headed to New York, as she flipped through the blank pages of the notebook Martica had given her for jotting down the contacts and friends she would make in her new life, Estefanía wondered again what might be behind Antonio's long silence. It had been weeks. He'd never answered the letter she sent him with the details of her trip, in which she repeated her interest in their Japanese tea and promised to bring him a sweet mango so he could experience for the first time what it was to drink the fruit's pulpy juice from a tear in its skin. Or the next one, in which she'd copied the first and asked if he'd received it. Or her last one, written just days before she arrived at her cousin Shirley's apartment in Queens. Had Antonio been scandalized by the image of a mouth sucking on a mango? Maybe it had stirred him in his strict celibacy. Had he been disappointed by the bourgeoise dolls, which Estefanía sensed were hardly worthy of an altar? Or maybe he'd had an accident. In his last letter, Antonio had mentioned a pain in his chest, terrible fatigue, and shortness of breath. That's why she was bringing him a mango. Martica always said that nothing kept a heart healthy like a mango.

The mango slowly rotted in Shirley's refrigerator. A few days after throwing it out, Estefanía went looking for the address Antonio had given her in one of his first emails. She took the Manhattan-bound subway Shirley had told her to and got off at Twenty-Third Street and Park Avenue. She walked along

Twenty-Third until she reached Second Avenue, then headed north to Twenty-Fifth. She passed a Laundromat, an Irish pub, the front steps of apartment buildings, and a storefront that announced itself as a Christian Science Library, but she didn't see a church anywhere. The building marked 228 was a pink multistory residence. Estefanía walked around the neighborhood looking for a church, but the only one she found was a few blocks away and had a sign out front that read, "FOR SALE. Immediate Occupancy."

She spent the next week visiting churches in Manhattan. She'd enter just as mass was ending, study the altar, and ask each priest if he knew Antonio Pesoa. The first churches were near the address he'd given her. But as she started visiting others further from the neighborhood, she realized she was going to spend the winter looking for him. And for the dolls.

On Halloween, Estefanía dressed up as a stray dog to go to the party Shirley had invited her to. A few gringos asked her to explain her costume, and she pointed to the sign hanging from her neck, which read, "Hello, I am a street dog (girl)" in her shiny new English.

—

Estefanía's ecclesiastical investigation came to an abrupt end in January, when Martica told her on one of their daily phone calls that she'd gotten a package from New York that had been sent to the clinic and then forwarded to her. Inside was a box wrapped in paper with drawings of monsters and Japanese characters on it, and a letter she read out loud.

Dear Estefanía:
I'm writing to let you know that Antonio Pesoa died at the end of September. As the friend in charge of distributing the objects he left behind, I wanted to inform you that I found this box in his apartment, ready for the post office and addressed to you (I hope this is still your address). He

spoke of you when he showed me the dolls he'd bought
from you. (I was the one who told him about the clinic;
I lived nearby when I was little. My mother brought several of my dolls there for repairs. It's a shame I never went
inside, though I always meant to.) Antonio would shut
himself up in his apartment with them for hours. He
didn't go out much toward the end. He didn't want to see
us because he was ashamed of his illness, so they became
his companions. He was working on a photo series of his
neighbors from the building sitting among the dolls and
parts you'd sent him. He told me a while ago that he was
writing an epistolary novel about a fugitive who hides in a
seminary on Manhattan's West Side and tries to find pieces
for the figurines in the adjoining church. In the novel
there was a girl who sent him those things from far away.
I haven't found the manuscript among his files, but if I do,
I'll make sure it reaches you. For now, I'm sending you this
package, which he left for you before his heart rebelled.
A hug from the friend of a friend,
Claudia Galindo

"Open it, Aunt Martica. What's in the box?"

"It's a book, sweetheart. An old book in who knows what
language."

The old leather-bound missal could only be opened to a
page in the middle; all the others were stuck together. There,
in a hollow carved out of the pages, the head of an antique doll
rested on a bed of dried flowers, protected under glass. A dark-
skinned face nested in a fragile book, surrounded by unfamiliar and unintelligible letters. Her eyes moved nervously back
and forth when the book was opened to reveal her.

In the photo of the gift that her aunt later sent, Estefanía recognized the head as Lucy's, the doll that had crossed the Seine
and then the Magdalena nearly a century before, in the arms of
a well-bred girl on her way to provincial Bogotá. The doll that

had declined the invitation to rot during its passage through the brutal heat of Honda, that had crossed the Andes on the back of a donkey, and that had withstood seventy years of being looked after by two upper-class women. Until Estefanía and Antonio came along to disrupt her years of peace and mothballs.

What had become of the other dolls, of the arms and eyes that found no place on any altar? When she buried her mother, Estefanía had come to understand that the living have trouble with the things left by their dead. Had Antonio's friends scooped them up and set them on their shelves? Were they in the window of some antiques shop? She even imagined them in a landfill somewhere outside New York, tiny arms sticking out from a mountain of plastic, old shoes, garbage bags, fruit rinds, office files, and computer screens. She thought of their little doll eyes fixed on the waste from silicone implants, syringes, yogurt cups, lunch boxes. Those antique glass eyes transformed into the inert filling of a dump in a country full of trash. Witnesses to the disintegration of bones from countless chicken wings that would decay faster than them. Eyes with no audience to witness the putrefaction they reflected.

She felt better thinking of the little head protected by the green leather binding of an old book that had made its way to Bogotá, searching for her.

"Aunt Martica, will you bring it with you when you come?"

The seven Claudia Galindos that Estefanía found on the internet—a beach volleyball player from Bogotá, a Mexican pastry chef, a Canadian lawyer, a sociology professor in Bolivia, an actress living in Miami, and others whose occupations were impossible to determine—never answered her emails.

—

With the exception of two weekends in February when snowstorms paralyzed the city, Estefanía spent every Saturday and Sunday that winter and spring visiting antique shops in

Manhattan in search of the other dolls. When her student visa expired early that summer and she needed to head back to Bogotá, she still had nine shops left on the long list she'd compiled for her pilgrimage. Lucy stayed behind, presiding over Shirley's apartment from her pagan altar. Estefanía promised them both that she'd be back soon and slid the list of the remaining antique shops into the book. So she could keep searching whenever she returned.

VARIATIONS ON THE BODY

*To take leave is to raise a dew for civil marriage
with the saliva.*

— José Lezama Lima, "Summons of the Desirer"
(tr. Nathaniel Tarn)

With her firm, fleshy hand, Martica pressed Mirla's fingers to her groin.

"Hold here."

The force with which the manicurist obliged her to touch her own privates always surprised her.

"Spread your legs a little wider, bring the right one up to the wall and pull this tight."

Martica stretched her client's wrinkled, spotted skin and dipped a stick into the hot wax, which gave off a smell of lemon. She applied the gummy liquid to the mounds where the old woman's buttocks began. For the past few years, it was only in those rare waxing sessions that Mirla had such a concrete awareness of those regions. She'd fallen out of the habit of exploring them.

Martica pursed her lips, the way she did when speaking to the dead Pekingese that adorned her living room with its taxidermized placidity.

"You're all skin and bones, Miss Mirla. Poor thing. I know you're sad, but you have to eat."

She rubbed the white linen strip she'd laid on the wax and pulled hard.

"I am a bit thin, aren't I? That's what Nora's been saying to me lately. She even makes the girl ask if I'm eating well. I think what I'm missing is dinners out with Pepe. Shit, Martica! Try not to leave me all red."

Martica tweezed the short hairs that remained, those few that still grew dark on her client's body at her age.

"There we go, you're all ready for the beach and your TV debut. Just promise me you'll eat better this week, you're wasting away."

Martica didn't believe that Mirla was going on vacation, as she'd claimed during their last two appointments. She probably said it to imagine how much she'd be missed, to find some ember of vitality. How was she going to take a vacation on what little money she had now that she was alone? She hadn't even paid for the last month of manicures, pedicures, and waxing, which added up. Martica hadn't charged her because she wasn't in the habit of invoicing anyone in mourning. She hadn't taken it very seriously, either, when Mirla asked her to put her in touch with a client who worked in TV, to see if she might be able to land a minor role in a soap opera. Martica had promised to give the woman a call, to see what they could do.

Mirla had been confused about certain things since Pepe's death. His children, who had always reproached him for talking about love at his age and for ending up with a Jewish woman, showed up at Mirla's house a week after the cremation announcing that they were going to take a few things that had belonged to their father—paintings, pre-Columbian objects, and pieces of colonial furniture that Pepe had gotten years earlier from the demolition of a convent in downtown Bogotá. Aside from a modest bank account Pepe had opened in both their names to save up for a trip to Curaçao in search of her ancestors, the only inheritance the deceased had left her was a bunch of knickknacks of questionable value that refused to relinquish their ghosts.

"Martica, did I show you my new pair of scissors? Do you think I'll be able to take them on the airplane with me?"

Ever since the tragedy, Mirla had been feeding a growing collection of scissors. As a businesswoman of the body, a cataloger of nails and hairs and cuticles, Martica couldn't grasp the appeal of a shiny pair of scissors beyond their utility. But, feigning curiosity, she applauded her client's initiative as a therapeutic strategy. In life, Pepe had collected collections. Mirla had spent entire sessions with Martica trying to figure out what to do with them. Should she keep the hundreds of matchboxes from all around the world, or should she give them away? And what about the watches that had belonged to generations of Valencias, the posters of old Hollywood movies, and—strangest of all, the one Mirla understood least because she'd never been steeped in the fetishes of Catholicism—a collection of nineteenth-century reliquaries that housed splinters of the bones of saints and beati? Martica had agreed that they might have market value. She'd even helped Mirla place an ad in the classifieds, but no one had showed any interest.

Martica spread perfumed talcum powder around the line of her client's satin underwear and made sure her tender skin was covered. She closed the jar of wax and began returning her tools for disciplining nails and cuticles to the cosmetics bag she brought with her from house to house for her appointments.

"But Miss Mirla, you don't even know what to do with the things Pepe left you when he died. Wouldn't it be better not to start a whole new collection?"

Martica regretted not having used a single diminutive to soften her words. She reminded her client that if her family was pressuring her to move from that sprawling home in a run-down neighborhood into a small apartment, it might be better not to go around accumulating so many things.

—

After the funeral, Mirla had ventured beyond the neighborhood a few times to search for old scissors in antique shops and jewelers. As she explained to Martica when she began sorting them, she was looking for all different types: shiny, adorned, old, specimens designed for a specific function. Above all, she wanted unusual scissors made for unimaginable, uncommon things. Like detaching from its pulpy muscle the finest clam, a delicacy in that Andean setting so far removed from her childhood. Or clipping the wings of parakeets and canaries that provided company for people at those high altitudes but longed to flap them in warmer climes. She wanted scissors that no longer served a purpose, that had fallen out of use in the absence of their objects, that missed the surface of their flesh. But she knew how hard those were to find, now that everything was made of plastic and dreary steel, now that a single pair promised to slice through anything, as the infomercials intoned. Despite these obstacles, Mirla had managed to acquire several specimens in the past month, some of them old and tarnished, others new and full of the promise of domestic utility.

Her most recent pair, the one Mirla valued above all the rest, had more or less fallen into her hands. It was a pair of surgical scissors, made of stainless steel, with long, thin blades, the kind used for invasive procedures, for removing tumors and other malignant flora. Mirla had been carrying them around in her purse since her trip to the hospital. She was convinced they would stand in for her arthritic hands when she needed to join the tips of her short, crooked fingers to pull on something small or loosen a knot. They would help her open the bag of peanuts she devoured when her taxi got stuck in traffic, or clip the fastenings of everyday objects. She was one of the many who believed in expressing discontent rather than swallowing it. In not letting it accumulate into little tumors. In cutting the vine rather than leaving it to strangle the tree. She had used many images like these to illustrate the idea over the years, but only now had she found the object that manifested her conviction.

"When someone or something gets under my skin, I stick my hand in my purse, grab my scissors, and cut the air. It works wonders. I imagine I'm cutting through the problem, and sometimes even that I'm cutting the person who's making me angry."

That was how she explained it to Martica, and how she'd explained it over the phone to Sophy, a cousin who had recently emigrated to Miami after a harrowing rash of kidnappings rattled several people they knew. Sophy had dismissed her metaphor and advised her to use the scissors to defend herself from the thieves she imagined lying in wait on every corner and behind every tree in Bogotá, plotting assaults in every nook and cranny of the neighborhood.

Martica finished putting away her manicure set. She concealed her desire to get out of there and studied the new specimen Mirla pulled from her purse.

"What a shame it would be if they took these from you at the airport, Miss Mirla, dear. They look expensive. And wouldn't it be a drag to get stopped for something so silly?"

Mirla thought about the green-gloved police officers who searched travelers in the women's line at El Dorado. She had always found them so mysterious. Maybe it wouldn't be such a bad thing if they got a little surprise. If they suddenly paused their coordinated opening of zippers and locks. If they stopped speculating about what might be inside suit case linings and stuffed animals. If they ignored their obsession with the powders they'd trained their dogs to sniff out. If they thought, for just a moment, about their hangnails, about their untrimmed pubic hair, about all the loose threads in their clothes, their days.

—

Mirla and Pepe met at that airport, standing at the window onto passport control and security, where people said good-bye to those who were leaving in droves. The crowd behind them pushed them into the glass as it tried to reach the front to send off its travelers.

"No one comes to this country, and just look at all the people leaving. Yet somehow the streets are always clogged with traffic."

Mirla had said it to no one in particular. A man standing next to her, waiting for his daughter to pass into the hygienic glare of the Duty Free, rushed to respond.

"You're absolutely right."

Pepe had already noticed the moisture in the creases around Mirla's eyes, the stalled engine in her throat. He watched her blow kisses to a young man, use a handkerchief to wipe the tears collecting in her mascara-heavy lashes, and run a fingernail under her lower lid to remove the dark sludge her makeup had formed there.

In a musty airport bar, over the first of many drinks they would have together, Mirla told the fellow with kind eyes and sunken cheeks that the young man she'd been saying good-bye to was "like a son" to her. Her nephew Pedro had lived with her for nearly a decade, ever since her sister Dora started passing him pamphlets for different therapies that promised to cure the disease of homosexuality. Mirla had given Pedro a set of keys so he could stay there whenever he wanted, and he ended up moving in completely. Dora stopped speaking to both of them. When he finished college, Pedro convinced himself— and Mirla—that he needed to move to New York. Mirla loaned him nearly all her savings.

"You can pay me back when you're a famous architect and fall madly in love with someone who treats you right."

But as she confessed to Pepe later that night, she knew the tourist visa Pedro had gotten for his trip to New York meant they weren't going to see each other for a long time.

"He doesn't realize it because I'm not old-fashioned, but I'm seventy years old. I could die any day now."

The afternoon Pedro left, Pepe asked for Mirla's telephone number after driving her home from the airport.

—

"They're surgical scissors, Martica. I didn't tell you before, but I bought them from a nurse at the clinic. She almost didn't sell them to me, she said they'd fire her on the spot if they caught her trafficking medical instruments. You have no idea how much money that woman got out of me, Martica, but tell me they aren't exquisite."

The day of the mass held for Pepe one week after his death, which she'd refused to attend, Mirla had felt shooting pains in her chest that doubled her over as Martica was giving her the first manicure of her widowhood. Martica drove her to the hospital, running every red light and stepping on the gas like never before. She waited for hours without news before they let her in to see Mirla in a hospital bed, surviving. Her eyes looked like melted gelatin, the skin of her face seemed thinner and glistened with sweat. A machine next to her translated the signs of her malady into a nervous melody.

Martica knew that Mirla needed a more satiating, less diluted kind of nourishment than what they were pumping through her body. She thought about how Pepe's death would keep ravaging her and that it might be better if Mirla began the process of letting herself slip away once and for all. She immediately reproached herself. She forced herself to celebrate her friend's survival and even congratulated herself for being there to save her.

The doctor explained to Martica and Nora, Mirla's daughter, that although cardiac failure was common among patients of Mirla's age, it was more likely that she was suffering from a more elusive, but no less real, condition. He called it broken heart syndrome. Martica knew Mirla would hate that name and promised herself to bring it up during her next manicure.

"Stress-related cardiomyopathy isn't a condition that can be treated surgically, strictly speaking. What we're dealing with isn't a question of blockages or pathogens. It's an emotional trauma that causes the brain to release high levels of stress hormones that end up paralyzing the cardiac muscle cells."

Martica believed the doctor. Though she specialized in things as transitory as the body's crests and crevices, she also knew a thing or two about its mysteries.

"She needs absolute calm. Calm and company. And it would do her a world of good to be down at sea level, a lack of oxygen stresses the organism even further."

Martica had stopped by Mirla's house the day after she got out of the hospital to see how she was doing and give her a foot cure (as Mirla called the sloughing and removal of dead skin and calluses that gave her a sense of existential relief every month).

"One grows so skeptical with age, don't you think, Martica? That whole business about broken hearts sounded like a load of nonsense to me. Some people find relief in their new solitude. But then there's all the cases you hear about, couples who are together for years—one of them dies and the other tries to follow them on the spot. Pepe and I, you know, we didn't talk about death much, but we did promise each other that once."

Martica responded with a similar story, about a client who died three days after her husband without even falling ill.

"You're my companion, my ambulance, my savior, Martica. Nora doesn't even believe I'm suffering."

Mirla had grabbed Martica's hand and was squeezing it hard. Martica grasped her spotted skin but didn't look up, for fear of meeting her client's watery eyes. She reached into the plastic tub for Mirla's right foot and pulled it out of the water with the force of a fishmonger grabbing a live mojarra to scale it. After studying the cuticles adorning the old woman's nails, she dug the orangewood stick under the deformed nail of her client's big toe and began to sculpt it.

Martica studied the newly acquired surgical scissors Mirla opened and closed in front of her.

"Be careful, those things are as sharp as a butcher's knife. Oh! I have to run, darling. It's getting late, and I have to get all the way across town. And you know how Seventh can get."

On her way to the door, Martica put on the fake-fur jacket she'd bought on her last trip to New York.

"You always look so elegant, Martica."

"Good luck with your granddaughter today. Be patient with her, it's a tough age. Don't forget she's nuts about you."

"Well, I suppose. But just look at how disagreeable that girl turned out."

"Call me if you need anything, okay? Day or night."

Mirla gave Martica a kiss, reminded her that she'd be waiting for her on Tuesday, and stood in the doorway until she got into her car.

In the kitchen, she poured herself a glass of wine. In her dressing room, she took off her robe and grabbed a purple bathing suit that was sitting on top of a pile of clothes. An Italian one-piece she bought in 1989 and that still looked new, though a long time had passed since then. She looked at herself in the full-length mirror. It hung loosely around her stomach and bunched a little near her pubis. It was true that her body wasn't as voluptuous as it had once been. She was bony, and the skin around her groin was irritated.

"Shit. I told Martica not to leave me all red."

She walked over to the unmade bed and turned on the television. *Decisions: Real-Life Stories* was on. Every time she'd watched an episode that past month, she'd imagined herself writing scripts for the show, bringing the stories of Martica's drug-trafficking clients to the screen. She adjusted the pillows under her head and took another sip of wine. She tried to fight off her drowsiness for a while then slid into a light sleep. A woman was getting a phone call about a tragedy just as she was returning from an afternoon at the beach. Soaking wet, her bathing suit showed its age. Mirla offered to cut the threads hanging from it, and the woman thanked her. She woke to the sound of a machine boring into the next street over. Her lips were crusted with red wine, and an acidic taste filled her mouth. She dialed Sophy's number in Miami.

"Sophy, this is the first time I've gotten your answering machine. I thought your English was better. Too bad I didn't catch you, I really need to talk to you. I won't be able to call for a while. I'm leaving. Everything's fine, it's nothing serious, don't go getting all worried, all right? I'll be fine, Sophy. *Don't worry*," she added in English. "I'll call you soon. Chao."

She went back into her dressing room and packed a weekend bag that had belonged to Pepe. Into it went a couple of skirts, a few blouses, sandals, and other light clothing for the lowlands that she found bunched up at the bottom of her drawers. She also threw in all her scissors and her mother's wooden box from Syria, where she kept Pepe's collection of reliquaries, then filled her cosmetics bag with all the creams that would fit inside. She set the alarm on Pepe's fifteen old watches for 11:00 p.m., the hour he had succumbed to his timeworn heart. She imagined their nocturnal wail accompanying him one month to the day after his departure, slicing through the emptiness of the house.

Those same watches announced that Karina's bus was about to arrive. As she crossed the street, she met eyes with Perki, the black dog who spent her days under the magnolia tree in the yard of the house facing hers. They'd become friends over the past year. Ever since Perki moved into that yard, Mirla went by every day to pet her. The two old girls had gradually perfected their routine. As soon as she saw her approaching, the dog trotted over and leaned against the fence that separated her from Mirla, who stuck her arthritic fingers through the gaps in the metal to grab her fur and scratch her belly. Perki would wag her tail and nuzzle Mirla's hand, unable to control the ecstatic movements of her flanks, which overcame her like electric shocks. Sometimes Mirla would open her purse and give her chicken bones or ribs. She always felt sad when the time came to leave Perki at the height of her excitement, the height of her wagging, begging for her endless company without any sense of how human time worked. They always promised to see one another soon. But Mirla knew that leaving and returning were things only she decided, and the injustice pained her.

She walked a block and quickened her pace when she saw that Karina was already getting off the bus on the corner.

"Grandma, you're always late."

The girl dropped her bag on the ground. Mirla slung it over her shoulder, and they headed to a park the next street over. Two nuns were sitting on a bench, and a few construction workers were resting on the grass in their stained uniforms. Mirla sat on one of the benches off to the side, where she could see her granddaughter out of the corner of her eye. As she always did, Karina climbed onto the rusted slide then headed for the swings and finished on the bars, where she practiced her arabesques and pirouettes every week. Mirla unfastened the buttons and opened the zippers of the little pink backpack. She found the school newsletters she'd read the week before, scrutinized the notes Nora had written to Karina's teacher over the past few days, and opened a notebook to the last page. There was a heart with a *k* inside drawn on it, and the words *Dear Enemies* written with clumsy penmanship, as if it were the opening to a letter. She was looking for something to prove that the girl was turning rotten. That her mother's mean spirit and rudeness were beginning to filter through into the child's things. Something to confirm that her granddaughter, with her eyes like an old woman's and her thick body, was going to end up just as hard and distant as Nora.

Mirla had studied Karina many times in search of some gesture, some piece or corner of her body—her chubby hands, maybe?—that might inspire a feeling of tenderness.

"It's like she was born hardened by the years."

She'd made this confession to Pepe and also to Martica, disappointed and angry at not having a granddaughter worthy of the love she'd been saving up over so many years to lavish on a child. Mirla had been on the verge of telling Martica that, since the girl was so chubby, she would take candies and chocolates out of her backpack and eat them herself, in secret. But she'd decided to withhold that part of her disclosure, like a parishioner who picks and chooses the content of her confession. The last thing she wanted was for her friend to see her as an insensitive old woman.

"Grandma, did you know that the eagle is a wild animal?"

Karina was shouting to her from atop the bars. Mirla pretended not to hear. She pulled the pink wallet from her granddaughter's little backpack and found two bills inside.

"You have a bird's name, don't you? A mirla is like a blackbird, right? Those are mean because they eat other birds. My mom showed me one in the garden the other day, it was all black with an orange beak and it was trying to attack a tiny little bird. I always shoo them off when I see them so they know they can't be in our garden."

Karina lifted one leg over her head and bent her knee around the bar.

"Mirlas are mean, yes. And you've never seen the ones in Curaçao. They have poisonous fangs, and they're even known to go after babies."

Mirla pulled the scissors from her purse.

"That's a big fat lie."

"I've seen them myself. There used to be lots of them in the garden at my grandmother's house."

"Look, Grandma, I'm the only one in my class who can do this trick."

She kicked her other leg straight out and spun once around the trembling bar.

"Me and a boy who can do bars and always wants to play with us. He's a pro at Olympic gymnastics, but everyone says he's weird and gross."

Mirla cut one of Karina's bills into little pieces and stuffed them back in her wallet. She crumpled the other one up and shoved it in her pocket.

When they got home, Karina went straight to the office to look through its drawers for ways to ease the boredom that spending a Friday afternoon in that house, which smelled like old things and where she wasn't allowed to watch TV, always produced in her. Ever since she could walk, Karina had rummaged through Mirla's drawers the way her friends did with their older sisters' belongings. With each passing year, she got a better sense of how all the things sprinkled around in different pieces of furniture went together. When she started school, her interest in finding the cash that sometimes floated around there had sharpened. She wanted to watch it accumulate in her new wallet, to fulfill her mother's often-repeated prophecy that her daughter had a real way with money.

Mirla left Karina to her investigations. In her dressing room, she took off her sweats and put on a pair of white linen pants whose wrinkles revealed her disarray, canvas shoes, and a blouse she'd always considered an elegant choice for the lowlands.

With suitcase in hand, she walked over to the export-grade roses that Pedro had sent to her the week after she got out of the hospital.

"Don't worry, you'll always be this gorgeous to me."

It made her sad to leave them there to experience their decay, with no one to put them out of their misery as they yellowed toward the end. She filled the vase with fresh water and stroked their petals then returned them to her nightstand.

She walked to the door carrying the suitcase so its wheels wouldn't make noise.

"Be right back, Karina darling."

The girl pretended not to hear her grandmother. Mirla latched all three locks on the front door from outside.

She hailed a taxi and asked the driver to wait with her suitcase before crossing the street to where Perki watched her, exuberant. They performed their routine. But this time Mirla let Perki lick her hand over and over with her slobbery tongue. It made her angry that she couldn't explain why she was leaving. The taxi driver hurried her along from the other side of the street. Mirla dug around her purse until she found her scissors, stuck them through a gap in the fence, and cut a few hairs from the lone white patch on Perki's chest. She stuck them in her bag. She hated knowing that what sparked her attack of melancholy wasn't the simplicity of Perki's life, but what it said about the complications of her own.

"I hope they take good care of you, my sweet girl. You'll always be this gorgeous to me too. Don't worry. We're going to be fine, both of us."

Mirla watched the dog's tail wagging and felt an icy sensation spread from her throat to the heart of her weariness.

The taxi brought her to the terminal after refusing to make a stop somewhere she could buy a bathing suit and threatening to charge her double for the ride. She got onto a nearly empty bus marked Expreso Bolivariano headed for Cartagena via Bucaramanga. She remembered that people advised against traveling on the highways at night because of the guerrillas' checkpoints. She found a seat for herself and her suitcase at the front of the bus and looked through her purse. She felt like she'd forgotten something at home, but she couldn't figure out what. There were her wallet and her address book. Her fingers brushed against the little surgical scissors and she took them out, shined them with the hem of her shirt, slid her fingers into their holes, and trimmed the strings she found dangling from the seat cover. She also took advantage of the moment to clip a few more threads hanging from the hem of her blouse.

Mirla woke in a sweat and tried to open one of the polarized windows, but it was stuck. She gathered that the bus was moving further into the heated intensity of the lowlands. She wanted the sickly sweet smell of humidity to force its way into her nose, but the bus's salvaged air prevented it. The sky was turning purple. She saw an empty fruit stand along the side of the road and two girls in school uniforms herding a few cows. On the narrow road that ran through the cultivated mountainside like a scar, the bus kept sticking its nose out, trying to pass the trucks. The threat of surprises around each upcoming curve complicated the attempt. It pushed its muzzle out and pulled it back in. It braked and accelerated.

Mirla studied the misty green backdrop of yarumo and guayacán trees, along with many others she couldn't name, bordering the mountains along the Suárez River. She recognized the yellow bells in bloom. But then the pasturelands and crops that interrupted the forest turned her thoughts to mortality (Pepe's, and that of the trees that once lived there and the insects banished from them) and she remembered Martica's recommendation not to expose herself to any stressful situations. So she decided to look straight ahead, focusing only on the road, like one of those horses who wear blinders because otherwise the panorama of the world would terrify them.

Mirla noticed a big red heart on the tarp covering the back of an eighteen-wheeler in front of them. A sign underneath proclaimed, in capital letters: I LOVE SOCORRO. She'd gone to Socorro decades earlier, on her way to the coast with her ex-husband and Nora. In the steeply inclined plaza presided over by the town's imposing stone church, they'd gotten stuck in the middle of a procession of buses, cars, and motorcycles that the priest had just blessed with holy water. As each car received the immaculate liquid, it honked its horn in electric excitement. Leading the cacophony was a bus full of children who shouted out its windows, delighted by the liquid grace that had just fallen over the vehicle. I LOVE SOCORRO. She was surprised by the sign's enthusiasm, which far surpassed her memory of the place. The bus passed another big rig with the same heart and slogan, on the verge of dissolving into the green darkness of the forest. The heart underneath the letters was plump, swollen. It was afflicted by a suspicious symmetry. Mirla took the liberty of ignoring that Socorro was a place and thought of what else the word named: help or aid. She imagined pot-bellied truck drivers, their faces and bodies hardened by the highways of the Andes and their manly big rigs, unabashedly proclaiming their need to be saved.

She'd planned to call Pedro in New York when she reached Cartagena, to invite him to swim in the soft seas of the islands like they had in 1995, when she brought him on a surprise trip to celebrate his eighteenth birthday and show him where his grandmother had disembarked from Curaçao at the beginning of the century. She examined her hands. She already had a few hangnails, which always happened when she traveled. She dug around in her bag for the scissors and tried to trim them. But the blades were too thick to grasp such delicate remains. Then she began to exercise her hand, which hurt the same way her heart did the day she collapsed; cutting the air around her, she told herself she'd feel better when she reached sea level, when she walked along the beach in Cartagena. Closing, opening.

"Hi, Martica. It's me. I'm sorry I didn't let you know, but I had to leave in a hurry yesterday. I'm calling to say don't worry about me. Everything's fine. I'm going to be out of town for a while, in Cartagena. Do me a favor, sweetheart. Nora's going to call you if she hasn't already, I imagine she'll be beside herself. Tell her that I told you I was going on a long trip but that I wouldn't say where. Try to calm her down. We don't need her making a fuss right now. Martica, I'm sorry I didn't say anything. I didn't want to get caught up in good-byes. I'll call you every few days to let you know what I'm up to, so you don't worry so much.

And I'm going to convince you to come visit me here. Okay. Take care of yourself, sweetheart. Bye. Bye."

Mirla ended the call. Then redialed.

"Hi, Martica. It's me again. I forgot something. Would you mind stopping by in a couple of days and leaving some scraps for the little black doggie who lives across the street from me? It's just . . . she's a friend of mine. Her name is Perki. She loves bones. Tell her they're from me, I wouldn't want her up and dying of sorrow on us. I'd really appreciate it, hon. Thanks. All right, I won't bother you anymore. I'll call you in a few days. Bye, now."

Mirla slipped the scissors back into her purse. She turned off her cell phone and paused to wonder how much she could get for it at a pawn shop. She would figure out soon enough how and when she'd have her cuticles trimmed, her groin pruned, and her nails, which were chipped from the hustle and bustle of this leg of the journey, painted again. And by whom.

Coffee House Press began as a small letterpress operation in 1972 and has grown into an internationally renowned nonprofit publisher of literary fiction, essay, poetry, and other work that doesn't fit neatly into genre categories.

Coffee House is both a publisher and an arts organization. Through our *Books in Action* program and publications, we've become interdisciplinary collaborators and incubators for new work and audience experiences. Our vision for the future is one where a publisher is a catalyst and connector.

LITERATURE
is not the same thing as
PUBLISHING

FUNDER ACKNOWLEDGMENTS

Coffee House Press is an internationally renowned independent book publisher and arts nonprofit based in Minneapolis, MN; through its literary publications and *Books in Action* program, Coffee House acts as a catalyst and connector—between authors and readers, ideas and resources, creativity and community, inspiration and action.

Coffee House Press books are made possible through the generous support of grants and donations from corporations, state and federal grant programs, family foundations, and the many individuals who believe in the transformational power of literature. This activity is made possible by the voters of Minnesota through a Minnesota State Arts Board Operating Support grant, thanks to the legislative appropriation from the Arts and Cultural Heritage Fund. Coffee House also receives major operating support from the Amazon Literary Partnership, Jerome Foundation, McKnight Foundation, Target Foundation, and the National Endowment for the Arts (NEA). To find out more about how NEA grants impact individuals and communities, visit www.arts.gov.

Coffee House Press receives additional support from Bookmobile; Dorsey & Whitney LLP; Fredrikson & Byron, P.A.; Kenneth Koch Literary Estate; the Matching Grant Program Fund of the Minneapolis Foundation; Mr. Pancks' Fund in memory of Graham Kimpton; the Schwab Charitable Fund; and the U.S. Bank Foundation.

THE PUBLISHER'S CIRCLE OF COFFEE HOUSE PRESS

Publisher's Circle members make significant contributions to Coffee House Press's annual giving campaign. Understanding that a strong financial base is necessary for the press to meet the challenges and opportunities that arise each year, this group plays a crucial part in the success of Coffee House's mission.

Recent Publisher's Circle members include many anonymous donors, Patricia A. Beithon, Anitra Budd, Andrew Brantingham, Dave & Kelli Cloutier, Mary Ebert & Paul Stembler, Chris Fischbach & Katie Dublinski, Jocelyn Hale & Glenn Miller, the Rehael Fund-Roger Hale/Nor Hall of the Minneapolis Foundation, Randy Hartten & Ron Lotz, Dylan Hicks & Nina Hale, William Hardacker, Kenneth & Susan Kahn, Stephen & Isabel Keating, the Kenneth Koch Literary Estate, Cinda Kornblum, Jennifer Kwon Dobbs & Stefan Liess, the Lambert Family Foundation, the Lenfestey Family Foundation, Sarah Lutman & Rob Rudolph, the Carol & Aaron Mack Charitable Fund of the Minneapolis Foundation, Gillian McCain, Malcolm S. McDermid & Katie Windle, Mary & Malcolm McDermid, Daniel N. Smith III & Maureen Millea Smith, Peter Nelson & Jennifer Swenson, Enrique & Jennifer Olivarez, Alan Polsky, Robin Preble, Jeffrey Sugerman & Sarah Schultz, Nan G. Swid, Grant Wood, and Margaret Wurtele.

For more information about the Publisher's Circle and other ways to support Coffee House Press books, authors, and activities, please visit www.coffeehousepress.org/pages/donate or contact us at info@coffeehousepress.org.

MARÍA OSPINA was born in Bogotá, Colombia, and teaches Latin American culture at Wesleyan University. She has written about memory, violence, and culture in contemporary Colombia. Her stories have appeared in several Colombian anthologies, and *Azares del cuerpo,* her first book of fiction, has been published in Colombia, Chile, Spain, and Italy. It is now available in English as *Variations on the Body.*

HEATHER CLEARY's translations include Betina González's *American Delirium,* Roque Larraquy's *Comemadre* (nominee, National Book Award for Translated Literature 2018) and Sergio Chejfec's *The Planets* (finalist, Best Translated Book Award 2013) and *The Dark* (nominee, National Translation Award 2014). A member of the Cedilla & Co. translation collective and a founding editor of the digital, bilingual *Buenos Aires Review,* she teaches at Sarah Lawrence College.

Variations on the Body was designed by
Bookmobile Design & Digital Publisher Services.
Text is set in Scala Pro.